MW00425504

THE EDGE OF
INSANITY

JAMESFLYNN

James Flynn grew up in Sidcup, Kent, England. He's taken on many roles in his life so far: juvenile delinquent, car paint sprayer, soldier in the British Army, twenty-something delinquent, lorry driver, part-time portrait painter, English teacher.

A lot of his time is spent scribbling on bits of paper to create stories, and when he's not doing that he sometimes likes to scribble on bits of paper to create drawings.

In 2017 he published his debut novel, *Conservation*.

All of his accumulated books and drawings can be found at:

www.jamesflynn.org

For my mum, Jeanne, who always encouraged
me to express my artistic side.

ACKNOWLEDGE-MENTS

All stories, drawings and poems in this book are my own creations. I would, however, like to thank the following for their help and support: Mark Hobbs for designing me a brilliant book cover (https://m.facebook.com/desksixtyfour/), Tracy Heath for her valuable feedback and support, DJ and producer LJHigh for letting me use his music for some promotional material (www.ljhigh.co.uk), and, last but not least, planet Earth, for aiding my imagination with your crazy, insane ways.

CONTENTS

PREFACE

These stories were written freely, with no intention on my part of creating something that fits neatly into a certain category or genre. When I create a story I try to make something unique and different, something hard to define.

My main objective, however, is to write the strangest, creepiest, weirdest tale I possibly can, something that'll get under the skin of the person reading it. I want my ideas to disturb and unsettle those who see them.

Have I achieved this with the stories contained within this book? Read on, and you can be the judge, jury and...executioner.

THE SKELETON CULT

A crazy, wild tribe, living amongst the trees

Their bodies torn and withered, from their heads down to their knees

They worshipped the man in the temple, serving him endlessly

But little did they know, of his actual identity

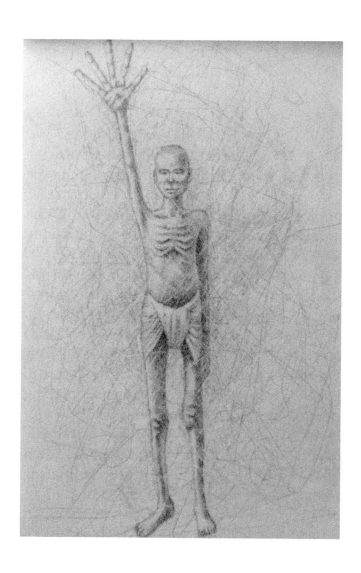

THE MESSAGE

Waves splashed and rolled onto the white sandy beach, dampening the soft grains, and wild palm trees sprouted up into the air further back from the shoreline, reaching for the faultless clear blue sky. The Andaman Islands are paradisiacal in every way, and this one was no different. It was a clique almost, an unspoiled stretch of natural habitat that would take anyone's breath away.

Further down the beach, however, things were a little more surreal. Rows of dark, skeletal bodies were assembled along the terrain, all standing upright and erect under the blazing hot sun. There were at least a hundred of them, all completely still, each one with a manic, delirious look in their eye with their spear down by their side. Identical in their posture, man or woman, each one held a bony hand high up in the air in a frozen salute. It was as though a pause button had been pressed, each and every one of them glued in position.

Had there been anyone around to observe this bizarre ritual, they would not only have been shocked by the apparent randomness of it all, but the sheer sight of their hands would've stunned them into a stupor. There was something very freakish and unnatural about their hands, for the fingers were excessively long and spindly, shooting up into the air like long, stiff tentacles. This was mirrored behind them in the form of a large monument sticking out of the dirt and sand, a bamboo structure with its own five digits. This elongated hand symbol clearly held some kind of importance for them, so much so that they'd tied twigs to their fingers to enhance their salutes.

A peculiar sound was resonating through the warm, humid air around them while they stood in their poses, coming from each of their mouths:

'hhhmmm...click...hhhmmm...click'

It was a deep humming sound, punctuated by a series of clicks. This, too, was obviously of some importance to them for they indulged in the activity with focus and perseverance, reeling off the hums and clicks with clear-cut precision.

This clan, this tribe, had been in their positions for hours, the various men and women holding their aching, withered arms up in the air the whole time, but they were nowhere near done yet. This frightful ceremony would continue until the sun sank down towards the horizon and the light faded away, and then, and only then, would they disassemble their frail, malnourished bodies, pick up their spears and disappear back into the thick tangle of trees from which they'd emerged.

△△△

Orange lantern light flickered and danced against the canopy of leaves in the heart of the jungle, causing an array of shadows to bounce and skitter about the place. Up above, through the gaps in the trees, stars twinkled against a jet-black sky. All eyes were on the large stone temple, its chunky steps and ancient blocks of masonry decorated with homemade lanterns burning brightly. The tribe's ceremony had now entered stage two, and they were lined up in a similar fashion as before but without their augmented fingers. Their arms were down by their sides now as they stood at the base of the temple steps, but they still stood with the upright posture of a grenadier guard. Hunger and fatigue was visibly eating away at each and every one of them, the whites of their eyes shot with red veins and their rib cages protruding out from their skin. It was close to 4am now and they hadn't eaten a thing all day, nor had they had much rest from the prolonged rituals they'd been putting themselves through. Every now and then a dull thud would interrupt the low cacophony of hums and clicks as a body hit the floor from exhaustion, a weakened member fainting after reaching their physical limit.

Upon close inspection there seemed to be something contradictory about the tribe; something about their appearance didn't make sense. Their skin reeked from the weeks-old grime and dirt that clung to it, their clothes were little more than rags, and their teeth and nails were falling apart, but every single member, females included, had neat hair that was trimmed to perfection. This inconsistency was odd, bordering on comical, as though they were imitating someone else's style.

Movement from within the temple caused a stir among the group. A figure became visible through one of the windows, a dark silhouette set against more lanterns that were flickering away inside. With slow, careful movements they walked onto the outside landing, paused for a few seconds, then made their way down the chunky stone steps towards the rows of delirious onlookers. The atmosphere around the temple had now completely transformed, and it seemed as though everyone was waiting for this mysterious person to speak. The man, tall and firmly built, looked out towards the assembled crowd with a blank expression, his smooth features smeared with dirt but otherwise faultless. Like the tribe before him, he too appeared to be something of an oddity. Grease clung to his skin and clothes, but he was otherwise well-trimmed and in good condition. A blond shock of hair was swept across his head, short and neat, and his features had a handsome beauty to them.

He looked out of place standing there under the jungle canopy, but it was clear that the tribe appreciated his presence and held him in an exceptionally high regard. Their cropped hair and rigid posture was obviously an imitation of his looks, and they stared up at him with silent expectation, the hums and clicks long subsided. When he eventually spoke it was in the tribe's own language and he spoke it with perfection, holding their undivided attention the whole time. And the message itself was surely very poignant, for there were gasps and cries of astonishment from all of the rows, with some people even breaking down into tears.

Once the speech was over the man turned on his heel, then walked back into the temple. As soon as he was out of sight, back in the depths of the old building, the clan broke out of their formation and fell into a state of disarray and panic, thrashing around like headless chickens. Their panic and anxiety was well justified, however, because they'd just been told that a very important visitor would soon be arriving on the island—and it was no less than god himself.

THE ARRIVAL

C has Youngham was gasping for breath by the time he finally managed to get himself over towards shallow water, coughing and sputtering. He was beyond exhausted and in a deep state of shock, his mind ablaze with traumatic thoughts and images. It looked as though he was safe for the time being, but just a few hours ago he'd witnessed his close friends drowning before his very eyes, so he was hardly in the mood for celebrating. They'd all been on a small boat, him and his three other backpacker friends from England, exploring some rocky caves around the Andaman Islands. They should never have gone out there, not without a guide at least, but in the spirit of young, twenty- something men they'd ignored the advice of the locals and ventured out to sea to do some amateur exploring. It'd gone well at first, and they'd impressed themselves with their rowing abilities, but as soon as they'd got close to the caves a series of submerged rocks and boulders had ripped the hull of the flimsy boat to pieces, throwing them all out into the unforgiving sea. His friends had died right there in front of him, but somehow, probably due to a mixture of luck and above-average swimming skills, Chas had managed to keep himself above water, eventually washing up on this island.

Wet, disoriented and bedraggled, he looked around and took in his new surroundings. The island had been nothing more than a blur to him as he'd approached it, a dash of green swishing across his peripheral vision as he thrashed around in the waves of the open sea, but now he could see it all clearly. Under better circumstances the place would have been beautiful, the unspoiled stretch of pearly-white sand cleaner and purer than anything he'd ever seen, but right now, in this terrified frame of mind, it looked no more welcoming than the raging ocean behind him.

The trees looked too dense and tangled to venture into so he instead traipsed along the stretch of beach, the scorching heat from the sun instantly drying his clothes. For ten minutes or so the only sign of life he could see consisted of birds and insects fluttering around the place, but this was about to change. The first thing he detected was a strange sound coming from around the gentle curve of the beach, somewhere just out of sight. He made his way steadily towards it, curious and intrigued. It was like a deep, continuous hum, flowing across the humid air in a low pitch, and the closer he got to it the more certain he was that it was human in origin. Chas stopped dead in his tracks when he saw the source of the noise.

When he saw the large assemblage of people lined up neatly in rows, his jaw dropped and his eyes grew wider. *The whole thing could be a mirage*, Chas thought, as he took in the giant hands reaching up for the sky. But he knew in his heart that this was not true; what he was seeing was very real, no matter how creepy and unsettling it was.

Things erupted very quickly. One of the scrawny-looking figures turned and spotted him, then alerted the others. Within seconds the tribe had dispersed from their neat, straight rows and were heading towards him, the sound of wild screams and wails replacing the deep hum. Fearing for his life, he turned and sprinted back the way he'd come, his feet sinking into the hot white sand in a nightmarish fashion. The race was lost before it'd even started, however, and he knew it. He was too exhausted to move quickly across the fine grains, too dehydrated to exert energy under the intense rays of the sun, and too baffled by what he'd seen to even concentrate on the task of running. He was on the ground when they reached him, collapsed and defeated. Hands began pulling at him from all directions, dark bodies looming over him and gripping his arms and legs. Chas began to scream and beg for his life, but his hysteria died down after a few moments when he realised that they were not trying to hurt him. They were armed with spears but they didn't seem to want to use them, they were too intent on hoisting him up into the air, cheering and laughing, apparently joyful of his presence on the island.

Dozens of palms probed him in a crazed frenzy as he was lifted up and carried away, voices squealing all around him in delight. He didn't put up a fight as he was whisked away towards the trees, he instead surrendered himself to this paroxysm of love and admiration, stretching out upon the carpet of hands in a mixture of wonder and befuddlement.

Lying there, seven feet above the ground with arms and legs akimbo, he watched the intricate network of leaves and branches pass by overhead, thankful for the shade it provided for his sunburnt skin. Brief waves of panic flushed through him every few minutes or so when he thought about the insanity of what was happening to him, but his fatigue plus the apparent benign nature of the crowd kept his fear in relative check.

He remained in this spreadeagled position for some time, hypnotised by the bursts of verdant foliage skimming by above his head, oblivious to the mutterings of the tribe in their foreign language. The experience had become so trippy and ethereal that the dreamy hand of sleep almost had him in its grasp, the ceiling of green coaxing him into unconsciousness like a lullaby to a baby, but just when he was about to give up trying to keep his eyelids open he felt himself slowing down. The terrain underneath him seemed to suddenly change, the many hands grasping him tighter and more firmly, and when he turned his head to see what was going on he was confronted by a huge temple standing ominously in front of him, its crumbling stone blocks half-consumed by the ivy and thorns of the jungle. The various men and women below him lowered him to the ground, steadying him as he found his feet, then pointed him in the direction of the tall, antiquated structure.

Before Chas even had a chance to get his wits about him he was being ushered up a huge set of steps, then coaxed into the building's shadowy interior. Once inside, he was encouraged to walk towards an elaborate-looking shrine on an elevated platform, which was embellished with numerous decorations. Chas looked up at this shrine through bleary, tired eyes, taking in the elaborate arrangement of lanterns and wooden ornaments. It also didn't escape his attention that a large hand-like symbol had been painted on the wall in an unknown substance, very similar to what he'd seen on the beach, but he was in no frame of mind to try and work out what it meant. With the roomful of people behind him still urging him on, he climbed up onto the shrine and sat down on the hard floor. Despite the complete lack of any cushions or bedding, there was no doubt in Chas's mind that he could sleep right there where he was, so he leaned back and stretched himself out on the floor. A series of confused gasps rang out across the room as he did so, however, and the sudden change in the atmosphere in the room told Chas that he was breaking some kind of cultural etiquette. He was far too tired to care, though, the long swim in the volatile ocean having drained him completely.

The last thing Chas saw before drifting off into a deep sleep was the sea of heads watching him from all four corners of the room, their sunken faces aghast. They were watching him with a frightening intensity, hardly taking the time to blink, their dedication and focus completely unfaltering.

△△△

Chas felt shaky and jittery when he woke up the next morning. His body had gone without food for twenty-four hours, and it was screaming out for nourishment. It took him a few minutes to fully regain consciousness, his eyes straining against the bright morning rays of sun beaming through the windows and cracks in the temple walls. When he felt ready and strong enough he sat up, leaning on one elbow, and looked across the room. For a second he thought he was still dreaming, seeing things that weren't there, his body tensing up with a sudden stab of icy fear. The natives were in their exact same positions, kneeling and sitting on the hard floor, watching his every move. Judging from the bags under their eyes and the gentle rocking of some of their heads, Chas had to presume that they'd been there all night, studying him as he slept.

Overcome with a sudden bout of stage fright, Chas was too scared to move. The dozens of gazes and stares were pressing down upon him, making him anxious and self-conscious, and he felt glued in position. Food and water was becoming an urgent need, however, so he fought through his nerves and fear and rose up to his feet, brushing himself off. He had yet to see anyone from the clan eat anything but he figured there must be fruit growing somewhere out in the trees, so he climbed down from the shrine and began walking towards the main temple doorway. His actions and movements caused his many admirers to murmur and fidget amongst themselves, and they shuffled around to clear a pathway for him. They then rose to their feet in his wake, grabbing their spears and following him out into the jungle like a herd of loyal sheep.

As Chas greedily gorged on fruit and berries, stuffing handfuls of them into his mouth, he could sense their surprise as they stood a few feet away from him and watched. *Do these people not eat?* he thought, glancing over at their withered forms. Their behaviour was a mystery to him but it wasn't going to stop him feeding himself, so he continued to eat until he could eat no more.

After his much-needed breakfast Chas walked back to the temple and spent the rest of the morning lying around by the temple steps, flanked on all sides by confused-looking tribe members.

MURRAY

As the days wore on Chas gradually began to feel revitalised. He created a loose routine for himself, sleeping for six hours each night, eating fruit and berries from the jungle during the day, and drinking rainwater collected in appropriately-shaped leaves. After studying the tribe for a longer period of time Chas realised that they did eat and drink, but they did so guiltily. They seemed to be more concerned about keeping their hair neatly trimmed than they did about keeping themselves nourished, but the exact reason behind this was still unknown.

Their reverence and admiration for him was never ending. The last thing Chas saw each night before he drifted off to sleep was a roomful of motionless forms silently watching him, and it was also the first thing he saw every morning when he woke up. The language barrier prevented any kind of deep communication taking place between them, however, and it was for this reason that Chas was completely oblivious for some time that there was a third party living in the temple. When he first heard the heavy footsteps echoing around an inner corridor one evening he nearly jumped out of his skin, and he was forced to swiftly investigate.

He was in his usual place when it happened, up on his decorative shrine, and he looked down towards the many faces looking for some kind of reaction. A plethora of questions ran through his mind upon hearing the sound: *Had the tribe heard it? Who could it be? Are they a threat?* It was dark, and the flickering shadows cast by the lanterns rattled his nerves and intensified his fear. There were entire sections of the temple that he hadn't yet seen, several rooms and corridors unexplored, and so as he followed the direction of the sound he was literally walking into the unknown. As always, he had his admiring followers just a few steps behind him, but they seemed to be more interested in watching him than protecting him.

The footsteps stopped after a few minutes, but Chas felt fairly confident that he knew where they'd come from. He turned a few corners, passing crumbling blocks of stone jutting out from the walls here and there, until he spotted a lit-up doorway in the distance. Putting one foot carefully in front of the other, he gingerly approached the illuminated room and peered inside. To his horror, a tall, well-built man was simply standing there, now completely silent and motionless. He was big and fairly stocky, his shoulders firm and intimidating under the soiled rags that hung from them.

Chas was instantly freaked out by the sight of him, his demeanour unusual and unsettling. He could only see the back of him from where he stood, but that was enough.

After one or two minutes he still hadn't moved an inch, and Chas actually began to wonder whether he might've fallen asleep standing up. But his eyes were open, he could just about see that from where he stood in the doorway, so he clearly wasn't asleep. *What's he doing? What's he looking at?* thought Chas, following the man's gaze towards the far wall of the room, where nothing was to be seen other than the crude, jagged brickwork. The entire room was empty, in fact, apart from a few dusty piles of rubble here and there; no furniture of any kind.

The sight of this stranger standing there had a peculiar effect on Chas, and after a while he could take no more. He edged away from the room as silently as he could, trying to keep his presence unknown. He suddenly wanted to leave the temple right away, to get away from this odd, intimidating man, but he also knew that he was effectively trapped inside of it. It was pitch black outside, and navigating through the unforgiving terrain of the jungle was simply out of the question. It was hard enough during the day, let alone during the night, and even if he somehow managed to make it to the beach in one piece he still wouldn't be able to go any further than that. He looked over towards his followers for some kind of guidance, some kind of clue as to who this man was, but received none; they just continued to crouch further along the passageway, quietly observing him as always.

Chas decided that he would have to remain in the temple at least until morning, but he would do so cautiously. If he slept at all, he would sleep light, keeping his ears peeled for any sound. He had the comfort of knowing that he wouldn't be alone, not with his crowd of admirers by his side, but whether they'd defend him or not if push came to shove he wasn't quite so sure. They all made way for him as he turned and headed back towards his shrine, their faces twisted with even more confusion than usual.

EPIPHANY

The next morning, Chas was too tired and anxious to eat. He would usually go out to pick fruit shortly after waking up, but he'd hardly slept a wink and he didn't feel up to it. Now that he knew that somebody else was residing in the temple, he could think of nothing else. At the first sign of daylight he'd hurried out of the temple just to get some air and think, and now he was sitting at the top of the temple steps. Just as he was wondering how the two of them had managed to avoid bumping into each other for so long, he heard slow footsteps behind him. When he turned his head he saw the man walking out of the temple entrance, a nonchalant expression spread across his smooth cheeks. Chas jumped up to his feet, worried that a confrontation was about to take place, but on the contrary the man hardly seemed to notice him. There was a brief look in his direction, a blank glance over to where he stood, but little more. In the bright light of day the man looked even stranger. He had a stiffness about him, an awkwardness that oozed from his movements and gestures. He also looked completely out of place on the island, at a total contrast to the natives.

There didn't seem to be much of a threat, at least not an immediate one, so Chas relaxed slightly as the man stepped towards him. A million questions still ran through his mind, though, the main one being whether or not the man spoke English. When the gap between them had been reduced to about two metres the man stopped, looking over at Chas with calm, expressionless blue eyes. A few seconds of uneasy silence passed, until Chas finally said:

'Who...Who are you?'

'My name is Murray.'

The man's voice really threw Chas off balance. His appearance was unsettling enough, but his voice was something else entirely. It was flat and emotionless, and didn't really fit the situation. There was no surprise in his tone, no curiosity at having met somebody else on the island, just a relaxed casualness like he was speaking to somebody on the street who'd asked for the time.

'And...do you live here on the island?' asked Chas, when it was clear that he wasn't going to get asked about his own name.

'The island is where I reside, yes.'

'Wh...What are you doing here?'

There was a brief pause while the man absorbed this question, his features completely unreadable.

'I'm here to study the local plants and fauna.'

'Really? So you're a scientist of some kind?'

Another pause, then, 'Yes, I study natural organisms.'

'Do you have a team with you? Any co-workers?'

'I conduct my research alone,' said the man, still looking at Chas with an expression that bordered on boredom. There was yet another brief pause, then he said, 'If you'll excuse me, I have to attend to certain matters.'

'Err, yes, of course,' muttered Chas, stepping aside so Murray could make his way down the big stone steps.

Chas was curious about the relationship between Murray and the tribe. He watched as the man walked down towards them all, strolling along with his big strides. The tribe were not panicked in any way by his presence, although they certainly acknowledged it. They moved over and cleared a path for him, allowing him to reach the wild thicket. There was noise coming from him as he walked off into the wilderness, some kind of muttering, but Chas could only hear snippets of it:

'...es...cour...err...es...of...cours...'

The encounter was baffling, and raised more questions than it answered. Murray was creepy to say the least, but Chas knew that he could be the key that he needed to get himself off the island. For days now he'd been pondering the idea of jumping back into the sea and trying to swim for help, but now he had another potential option at his disposal. He would stay put for now, he decided, and try to work out exactly who Murray was, and whether or not he could help him return to civilisation.

△△△

Murray was not an easy person to get close to, however. His reserved and elusive nature made him hard to watch, let alone approach, and the more Chas tried to do so the more he understood how he'd managed to go so long without even being aware of his presence. He had a regular routine in place, leaving the temple every morning to venture into the jungle, then returning shortly before nightfall, but socialising certainly didn't seem to be at the top of his agenda. The man was content in his own little world, going about his daily jobs and tasks with little concern about anything else.

After a few unsuccessful attempts at conversation, Chas decided to follow Murray during one of his walks through the jungle. Waiting patiently by the temple steps one morning, he let Murray walk off into the foliage then trailed behind him, just out of sight. While this espionage mission was taking place Chas had his own followers trailing behind him of course, but they were all far enough away from Murray to remain unseen. For about an hour or so he watched on as Murray trudged around the uneven terrain studying plants and leaves, gazing towards the various organisms with his blank expression. It was odd watching him work, painful even, such was the sheer awkwardness of the man. It didn't escape Chas's attention either that he had no equipment with him. At no point did he take notes or photographs, and Chas wondered why this was.

After a while Murray walked out of the thick growth and headed towards the beach. Chas was confused about this at first, but he reasoned that there must've been plenty of life in some form or other out by the shore. Keeping a safe distance away, he continued to follow him towards the sunny beach with the clan close behind. The sound of splashing waves became detectable and the light penetrating through the trees became more intense, but Chas stopped by the edge of the tree line, refraining himself from walking out onto the sand. He didn't want Murray to see him, and he was much more well-hidden in the trees than he was on the beach. Crouching down in the dirt, leaning against the thick trunk of a kapok tree, he peered out at Murray as he walked out into the sunshine.

A few seconds later, Chas couldn't believe what he was seeing.

Murray was standing directly in the glare of the sun, showing no sign of discomfort whatsoever, when suddenly he raised his right hand high up into the air. Chas instantly recognised this gesture to be similar to the one he'd seen the tribe do countless times before, but things were about to get even stranger. Once his hand was up in the air in a fixed position, Murray's fingers began to stretch and grow. Chas watched in shock and horror as all five digits became elongated, pointing up towards the clear blue sky like sticks. He actually rubbed his eyes a few times while this was going on, convinced that he was seeing things, but every time he looked back towards Murray he saw exactly the same thing. Each finger was about three feet in length, protruding from his palm like a long stiff twig; it was completely abnormal, sending shivers of revulsion up and down Chas's spine as he watched on, open- mouthed. But as his eyes adjusted to the light he realised that the fingers weren't made of flesh, they were made of metal. They glistened and reflected the rays of the sun, shining brightly like polished steel rods. A series of clicking noises became detectable during this time, as did a strange humming or whirring sound, similar to a large computer being booted up.

Chas's heart was doing somersaults in his chest as a chilling epiphany came to him: Murray was a droid. Suddenly, everything made sense. The tribe's entire culture was based on Murray. Everything they did was an imitation of his actions and behaviour: the hand-like structures, the hand-like paintings on the temple walls, the ritualistic salutes, the humming and clicking noises, and even their neatly-trimmed haircuts. But there was even more to it than that. Chas looked over his shoulder towards the clan members crouched behind him, taking in their protruding bones and tired, bloodshot eyes. They were depriving themselves of food and sleep because they never saw Murray doing it, obviously because he himself didn't need to. At some point, Chas concluded, Murray had been put on this island and the tribe saw his abnormal features as god-like, eventually worshipping him and adjusting their way of life accordingly. This revelation was enormous, but two questions still remained: firstly, who put Murray on the island? And secondly, why were the tribe now worshipping him instead of Murray?

He looked back out towards the white sandy beach, where Murray was still standing with his hand raised up above his head. The fingers were clearly aerials of some kind, used for transmitting or receiving signals. And if Murray was picking up or sending signals in this way, Chas thought, that meant that somebody somewhere was communicating with him. The more Chas pondered this the more he saw it as a potential way to get off the island, and it reignited his hope. Murray had been built by someone, and whoever they were, or wherever they were, they'd eventually want to come and collect him. Chas didn't know whether Murray's makers were friendly or not, but his situation wasn't ideal anyway so he didn't have much to lose.

He thought about walking out onto the beach and approaching the droid, but decided not to. He looked unresponsive out there, even more so than usual, shut down to perform this specific task. With a newfound sense of optimism, Chas climbed to his feet and returned to the temple, the various tribe members following suit. Murray was definitely going to be his ticket out of there, but first he had to work out how he was going to set it all into motion.

MURDER

The sun was low in the sky, sending warm orange rays through the gaps in the trees. There was a mellow atmosphere around the temple, too, the tribe silently sitting and watching Chas as he chewed on some berries. Chas was patiently waiting for Murray to return from one of his walks, ready to confront him and ask him some questions. He'd been holding back all week, hesitant to say anything to the droid for fear of his words being transmitted to some unknown foreign source, but now he didn't care. He had to find out who made the robot, and he wanted to see if he could extract the information from it verbally. When he came stomping out of the bushes Chas rose to his feet and blocked the steps, firmly standing his ground.

'Who sent you here, Murray?'

The droid stopped a few feet away from Chas, moving his synthetic lips. 'Who sent you here, Murray?'

'Answer the question,' spat Chas.

'I'm conducting solo research.'

'Yes I know, but who sent you here?'

'That's an interesting question. Unfortunately, I don't think I have an answer for it right now.'

Murray walked around Chas and proceeded to walk up the stone steps, forcing Chas to turn and follow.

'Wait! Don't just walk away! Who made you, Murray? You're a droid. Who built you?'

'I apologise, but I'm afraid I can't assist you with this matter.'

'Apologise? Apologise?! I'm stuck on this fucking island for crying out loud! I need some fucking answers or something! Anything! Please!'

'I will consider your request and get back to you as soon as I can,' said Murray, still climbing the steps.

'Who do you communicate with while you're on the beach?'

'Who do you communicate with while you're on the beach? Who do you communicate with while you're on the beach? Who do you...'

Chas gave up. He watched Murray disappear into the shadows of the temple, repeating his question over and over again. Once the droid was out of sight, he turned to walk back down the steps. He didn't get further than two paces, though, before coming to an abrupt stop.

The entire clan was gone, vanished. The large patch of ground where they'd previously been sitting was completely empty and Chas looked across it, puzzled, in the manner of a distraught child who'd just lost his parents at a fairground. At some point during his angry encounter with Murray they'd all got up and scarpered, but he'd been too fired up to hear or notice anything. 'What the hell?' he muttered, gazing around in complete bafflement. It was the first time they'd left his side ever since he arrived on the island, so whatever it was that made them dart off must've been very significant. As he was scratching his head, trying to work out which direction they'd gone, a faint noise reached his ears. It was coming from straight ahead, from the thin pathway that led towards the shore, and it sounded like the cries and yells of a mass brawl. Without a moment's thought Chas took off in that direction, eager to find out what the hell was going on.

The shouting and chanting grew louder as he ventured through the dense habitat, and by the time he got to the beach it was deafening. A big cluster of bodies were out by the shoreline, all thrashing around in a state of panic, and it soon became clear that some kind of fight was taking place. Chas's initial thought was that a scuffle had broken out between two members of the tribe, but when he spotted the small boat floating behind them all, rocking and bobbing on the waves, this theory was blown apart. Someone else had arrived on the island, and they were being beaten to within an inch of their life.

It was a lone man, lying on his back near the edge of the water, his arms and legs curled up in a defensive pose. An onslaught of kicks, punches and spear stabs were raining down upon him, coming at him from all sides, and he was powerless to stop it. His agonised pleas for mercy were drowned out by the bloodthirsty screams of the tribe, and the resulting sound cut through Chas like a cold knife. Even from a sizeable distance away the carnage was too much to bear, the level of violence almost animalistic in its nature.

After a few minutes the man ceased struggling, and fell back limply against the damp ground. But the brutality didn't end there. Even after the man had died, four members of the clan each grabbed an arm or a leg and lifted him above the ground, holding him firmly. Then, as Chas watched on through gritted teeth, they pulled and heaved at the man's limbs, tearing them off one by one. Once the man had been reduced to a limbless torso, his assorted body parts were then thrown out to the frothy sea, left to drift away into the wide blue yonder alongside his empty boat.

Chas had seen enough. He sprinted back into the seclusion of the trees, shaken and stunned by what he'd just witnessed. He was running, but he didn't really know where he was going. *Was he still safe here on the island? Had the tribe flipped? Was he next? Would they turn on him now?*

His body was a bag of fear and adrenaline bouncing along the dirt path, and he'd lost all coordination and rhythm. The exposed tree roots and contours in the ground that he usually stepped over with ease were now causing him to trip and stumble, and he was struggling to remain on his feet. He fell towards the floor, tears of frustration streaming from his face, wincing from the pain of the impact.

When the tribe appeared behind him, heading his way fast, he braced himself for whatever might've been coming his way. They were upon him in seconds, flanking him from both sides, and Chas curled up in defence. But the attack that he was expecting didn't come. Hands reached and grasped at his arms and legs but they did so out of hospitality, carrying him because of his injury. Chas tensed up as the tribe lifted him and carried him like they'd done when he first arrived, feeling as though he was caught in the grip of a pack of murderers. They were now cast in a different light to him, their withdrawn faces taking on demonic forms.

But it was also clear that they meant him no harm. As he was carried horizontally through the jungle once again, drifting upon a cloud of hands, the fear for his own safety diminished. They had all just committed an act of brutal murder but they'd done it to protect him, and now, in a final act of loyalty, they were carrying him back to safety. Chas's head span from the emotions and thoughts bearing down on him. *Who was the man on the beach? Did he really pose a threat, or was he killed for no reason? And if he did pose a threat, did that excuse the tribe's actions?* In terms of immediate practicality, only one thing really mattered to Chas now: he was, for the time being, safe. If the man on the beach was connected with Murray his chances of making it back to civilisation had been seriously impaired, but at least he was still safe for now.

ODDBALL

I t was late in the afternoon, and the Indian Maritime Search and Rescue Team were about to call it a day. The light was beginning to fade, the sun nothing but a faint red-orange glow on the distant horizon, and despite searching the waters around the Andaman Islands all day they still hadn't found the fourth backpacker. The search had been going on for weeks now, with daily patrols being sent out around the relevant areas, but nothing had turned up. The other three bodies had revealed themselves straight away, floating near some rocks by the mouth of a cave, but the fourth one was proving itself to be hard to find. There was a possibility that the young man was still alive, of course, but every member of the rescue team doubted this. They all understood the rough nature of the Indian Ocean, the sheer force of the waves and current, and the man would have had no kind of life-saving equipment with him whatsoever.

'OK, let's turn around and head back,' said the search team leader, a burly-looking man in his mid-thirties. 'There's nothing here.'

The skipper nodded briefly, then spun the inboard diesel rescue boat around with experienced dexterity. They'd travelled no further than fifty metres back in the direction of their base, however, when one of them spotted an unusual-looking object bobbing along across the waves.

'What's that?' shouted one of the team personnel, leaning over the edge of the boat.

'What's what?' said the team leader.

'That! Over there!'

The search team leader recoiled in horror when he finally saw it, then ordered the skipper to stop the vessel. Just a short distance away from them, right there in plain sight, a limbless torso was floating on the surface of the water. The belly was bloated, the mutilated stumps showed exposed flesh and bone, and the sagging head was pale and ghost-like. There was a moment of unease amongst the team as they squinted down towards the wet carcass, taking in the ghastly sight, and during that moment they all realised the same thing: this was no longer an accident investigation, it was a murder investigation.

ΔΔΔ

'So, what are we dealing with here?' said Metropolitan Police Chief Inspector Beckett, looking over his desk towards the constable who'd been researching the situation.

'The murder victim is a Mr Terry Crandall. An apparent eccentric loner who was living on the outskirts of South London.'

'Is he connected in any way to the missing backpackers?'

'No, sir. Indian authorities contacted the man who hired out the boat to Chas Youngham and his friends, and he didn't see anyone matching Terry Crandall's description.'

'OK, it could just be a coincidence that they're both English,' said the inspector. 'And we're completely sure that Crandall's injuries were not sustained at sea?'

'Yes, sir. The pathologist confirmed that the injuries were not caused by a shark attack, or anything like that.'

'Right, so it's definitely a murder investigation.' Inspector Beckett scratched his chin in contemplation. 'Has Chas Youngham been found yet?'

'No, he hasn't. The bodies of his friends have been found, but he's still missing.'

'What did the pathologist have to say about Chas's friends?'

'The official report cites drowning as the causes of death. No foul play suspected.'

'Alright, what do we know about this Terry Crandall?'

'He was a strange one, sir. A bit of an odd-ball. His house is full to the brim with odds and ends: tools, electrical equipment, computers,

41

you name it. He even converted a couple of rooms into workshops.'

'What did he like building?' asked the inspector.

'Gadgets,' said the constable, after clearing his throat. 'And...'

'And?'

'Well...robots.'

Beckett sighed. 'Go on.'

'We've been through all of his stuff, notebooks, photographs, everything, and it's very clear that he built some kind of robot, sir. Or droid, as he refers to it in his notes.'

'And what do we know about the droid?'

'We know that it's very advanced and sophisticated. I have no idea how he managed to develop this thing on his own, but the evidence suggests that he did, and it's very good. His hard drive is full of videos recorded by the droid, and —'

'Videos recorded by the droid?'

'Yes. It appears that he sent, or took, this robot to one of the Andaman Islands to gather information. There's still loads of footage that we haven't seen, but we think we've worked out what's happened.'

'Yes?'

'Terry Crandall appeared to have an obsession with these islands, sir. He wanted to study everything, the plants, the animals, the natives, and he used his droid to do it.'

'Why didn't he just do it himself?' asked the chief inspector, looking baffled by everything he was hearing.

'Certain tribes around the Andaman Islands are notoriously hostile, sir. They've been known to attack visitors. Maybe he used the robot for his own safety.'

'Do we know which island this robot's on?'

'Yes. The Indian authorities have identified it using some of the footage we sent them.'

'How did Crandall get the robot there?'

'That, we don't know, but he certainly managed it somehow. And once it was there, he let it do all of his dirty work for him. And this is where it gets strange, sir.'

'More strange than it is already?' sighed Beckett.

'Yes, I'm afraid so. The natives of this island must've been of particular interest to Mr Crandall, because he made a massive effort to try and communicate with them.'

'He tried to communicate with the natives through this...droid of his?'

'Yes. And he was very successful, too. He was able to learn the tribe's language.' The constable thought for a moment. 'Or maybe it was the robot who did that, we don't know yet. But either way, he spoke to them via the droid. And...well, the thing is, sir...'

'Go on. Spit it out,' said Inspector Beckett.

'This tribe...well, all of the evidence suggests that they worshipped the robot. When it appeared on the island they'd obviously never seen anything like it before, it was completely new to them, and over time they began to see it as magical. They thought it'd been sent down from the heavens, or something.'

'Bloody hell, I've heard it all now!' said Beckett, holding his head in his hands.

'Crandall must've seen an opportunity here, sir, because he used the tribe's reverence of the robot to his own advantage—or at least he tried to. When he saw what was going on, he sent a special message to the tribe via the robot.'

'A special message?'

'He ordered his robot to approach the tribe and tell them that he, or it, was not the one they should be worshipping. The message stated that the real, ultimate god would soon be arriving on the island, and they should worship him instead.' The constable leaned back in his chair. 'This was all delivered in the tribe's own language, of course.'

'And this so called god was Mr Terry Crandall himself, I take it?' grumbled the inspector, rolling his eyes.

'Yes. Crandall was trying to set himself up as a god on the island. He saw how much they admired his robot, and he was trying to divert that admiration towards himself. From what we can see, sir, the man was a reclusive loner.

He had no girlfriend or wife, his house is like an electrical junkyard, and according to his neighbours he seldom went out. Who knows, maybe he was jealous of his robot? Maybe he saw it as an injustice that the droid was appreciated and loved, while he himself was festering away in the darkness of his cold house?'

Inspector Beckett rubbed his eyes and took a deep breath. 'So you're honestly telling me that this man falsely convinced a tribe on the other side of the planet that he was some kind of supernatural being, and then actually tried to travel over to them to let them worship him?'

'That's my personal conclusion, yes. And it's backed up by lots of evidence.'

'How did he get there?'

'By plane and by boat. We've been through all of his emails with a fine-toothed comb, and we've found plane ticket receipts and an invoice for a boat he hired from somewhere in India.'

'So why was he killed? Why did his body turn up floating in the sea with missing limbs?'

'This is what we still haven't worked out, sir. Anything could've happened, though. He could've been intercepted on route and attacked by pirates, or he could've been killed on the island and then thrown back out into the sea.'

'Killed on the island? But the tribe would've wanted to protect him, wouldn't they? Not kill

45

him.'

'Exactly. That's what makes me think that he may have been intercepted on route to the island.'

The chief inspector's face suddenly dropped.

'What is it, sir?'

'Is this robot still sending videos back?'

'Unfortunately not. We think that Crandall may have sent it a command to stop relaying videos the day he left England. He probably didn't want anybody to know where he was. Why do you ask, sir? What is it?'

'You don't suppose this Chas fellow...'

Inspector Beckett trailed off, the idea swirling around in his mind stunning him into silence. Once he'd had a moment to recompose himself, he looked over at the constable and said, 'Find the commissioner's direct extension. We need to get someone over to that bloody island right now!'

DEADLY FACE-OFF

C has gazed out towards the sea of obedient faces before him, a warm smile spread across his cheeks. He was sat on his shrine, casually leaning on one hand, happy and peaceful within himself. The dust had long settled from the attack on the beach, and he'd started to see the whole thing in a different light. There'd been a change of outlook, an adjustment of his psyche, and he no longer saw the tribe's actions as deplorable. Their actions that day had been for him, all for him, and he had no choice but to acknowledge that and be grateful. The incessant love and servitude that oozed from them had consumed him, encircling him in a constant haze.

For a long time Chas had puzzled over the source of this love, wondering where it all came from, but it just didn't seem to matter anymore. The only thing that mattered to Chas now as he sat up on his elevated platform, basking in the mellow vibes, was that he had the tribe and the tribe had him. The island was his home, the temple was his house, and the tribe were his family; nothing outside this seemed to matter anymore. The problems and questions had grown distant, becoming dim and insignificant, the urgency and importance losing its edge. He was living in a world of contentment.

This contentment was suddenly smashed, however, when a loud noise echoed in from outside. The sound caused everybody in the room to jolt, instantly altering the atmosphere of the room. All heads turned towards the main doorway where a withered tribesman stood panting for breath, exhausted after having run back from the beach. He was shouting in between each painful gasp, trying to convey something. Chas was yet to fully grasp the clan's dialect, but there was no mistaking the general message that was being put across: trouble had broken out again, and assistance was needed.

The masses shot straight up to their feet, ready to defend their deity once again, and pelted outside. As this unexpected commotion was taking place Chas was overcome with a strange sense of intuition, and he knew at once what was going on. They'd found him; the outside world knew where he was, and somebody was out there to collect him. This realisation had a peculiar effect, putting him into a strange dilemma: should he listen to his brain, which was telling him to run to the beach and climb aboard whatever rescue boat was there waiting for him? Or should he listen to his heart, which was telling him to stay with his loving, loyal followers? Abandoning the island now would be akin to abandoning his family, turning his back on the ones who'd killed for him, but staying there would be akin to pure insanity.

He walked outside then halted by the top of the temple steps, watching the men and women sprinting away towards the shore, spears in hand. His mind ached from the predicament that he was in. Should he stay, or should he go?

△△△

When the rigid-hulled inflatable boat reached the shoreline, the handful of elite soldiers jumped straight out. Dressed in black, they were highly visible against the white sand of the beach, but their mission was not supposed to be of a covert nature. Their orders were to collect Chas Youngham by any means possible, then get the hell off the island. Rifles at the ready, they trudged across the hot sand, their skin clammy with sweat under the thick protective layers of their uniforms.

It didn't take long for the natives to show up. They emerged from the greenery, spears in hand, ready to attack their unwanted visitors. A deadly face-off soon broke out along the stretch of beach, with the two opposing factions confronting each other with their own style of weaponry. The sweltering air was tense and heavy, thick enough to taste. Things were about to erupt, fingers squeezing triggers and hands gripping spears, when there was movement from further down along the tree line. A figure walked out onto the sand, calm and fearless, and turned to face the soldiers.

'I'm Chas Youngham,' he said. 'Let's go.'

Nobody dared take their aim away from the tribe, but the commander called over to Chas, shouting out of the side of his mouth.

'Walk slowly towards us, Chas. No sudden movements.'

Surprisingly, the tribe didn't seem fazed as he stepped towards them, and once they had him in a safe position they ushered him towards the inflatable boat, rifles still cocked and aimed. Within seconds they were all aboard and the helmsman started the engine, steering the boat back out into the Indian Ocean.

The island shrank to a thin slit on the horizon as the rigid-hulled vessel soared across the open sea, fountains of fine white spray shooting up behind it. Now that the tense ordeal was over the special forces team allowed themselves to loosen up and relax a little, switching on their safety catches and leaning back in their seats. The commander turned towards Chas, noticing how quiet and distant he was. The young man was clearly in a state of shock, blankly staring out towards the waves, in need of some support. The commander had dealt with traumatised victims before, and he knew that it was better to get people talking rather than letting them sink back within themselves, so he attempted to coax Chas into some light conversation.

'So, tell me about what happened. What have you been doing on that island all this time?'

The question hung in the air for a long moment. So long, in fact, that the team of soldiers on either side of the boat looked up at each other uncomfortably. Then, in a controlled, slow monotone, the answer finally came:

'I was there to study the local plants and fauna.'

△△△

Chas crouched in the cool shade of the trees as the soldiers sped away in the distance, a mere speck on the vast rippling waves. He felt sad to see Murray go; he'd miss him, he knew he would. Communication and dialogue with the droid had been limited to say the least, but he'd held a certain presence on the island nonetheless.

When the boat finally vanished Chas looked behind him, back in the direction of the teeming vines of the jungle. His loyal family was scattered around the terrain, watching him with the usual fondness and wonderment. He was still none the wiser as to why they held him in such high esteem, but there must've been a good reason for it, he thought to himself, as he walked back into their embrace.

THE UNBORN

He was a junky boozer, wasting away his days

The lowest of the low, lost in a drug-fuelled haze

But then he had a visit, from unexpected guests

They knew him inside out, and put him to the test

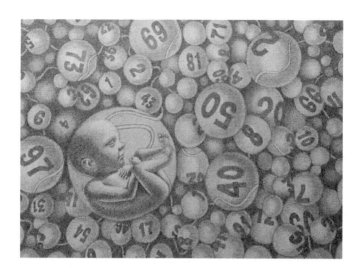

S tanley sat slouched on the torn sofa, a fog of cigarette smoke hanging lazily around his head. Opposite him, one of his cronies was gulping down the last mouthfuls of warm, flat beer from a can.

'We're out of drink,' he said, crushing the empty can in his hand and then throwing it down onto an empty crate by their feet.

'Who's turn is it then?' came another voice from the kitchen.

The question caused a tense silence to hang in the air for a moment, but then Stanley felt all eyes upon him as his two friends faced his way, one from the sofa opposite him and one from the doorway of the kitchen. He didn't bother putting up a fight, for he knew fair well that it was his turn to walk round to the late-night off-licence to do a beer run. Closing his bloodshot eyes he sighed in submission, accepting the fact that this arduous duty had to be carried out.

Beer run duty was inconvenient, but not because he had to spend any money, it was inconvenient because it involved walking into the store, picking up a crate of beer, and then pelting out of the door as fast as his legs could carry him, hoping that the shop owner wouldn't bother taking chase.

'Come on Stanley boy, get your jacket on,'

said his wide-eyed acquaintance from the kitchen doorway, with a shark-like grin spread across his face.

'Alright, alright,' muttered Stanley, climbing to his feet and kicking his way through the cigarette butts, cans, and takeaway boxes that littered the carpet.

'You can even have a livener before you go. How about that?' called the voice from the kitchen, amidst the sound of a card tapping against a glass surface.

Walking past his semi-conscious friend on the sofa, he entered the kitchen where he was passed a rolled-up bank note.

With his nostrils still stinging, Stanley marched down the road towards the late-night shop with an edgy spring in his step. He was particularly anxious tonight for two reasons: firstly, he'd done so many beers runs from this area that the shop keepers now knew his face, making his job twice as risky. Secondly, the last time he'd walked under the flyover that he was now approaching, he'd ended up in a nasty confrontation with a crazed homeless man who'd jumped out at him from the shadows, grabbing him by the scruff of the neck.

It'd happened a week ago. He'd been heading over to his friend's squat with a stolen laptop late in the evening, and as he was passing under the bridge in the dark, a crazed, grotty-looking, hooded man pounced on him from the shadows, blocking his path. His initial thought was that the man's intention was to rob him of the laptop, but it soon became clear that that wasn't the case. Instead, he'd seemed hell-bent on having a drunken rant, yapping on about something that didn't even seem to make any sense.

'What the fuck are you doing?' Stanley had yelled, as the man's knuckles pushed against his neck and chest.

With his face completely hidden in shadow, the voice that seeped out from beneath the hood had been grave and intense.

'I'll give you one week to turn your life around. One week to start appreciating what you've got.'

Half choking, Stanley replied, 'What the hell are you on, you freak?! Get off me!'

'One week,' said the voice from the shadows. 'No more.'

If it hadn't been for the fact that he'd had a laptop computer in his hand and fifty quid waiting for him down the road, he would've swung for him, but he'd been more keen to sell his stolen goods at the time than stand there with some nutcase. Later that night, after several beers and lines of cocaine, he'd forgotten all about that little encounter, but now, as the flyover came into sight just up ahead of him, it all came flooding back. With no other way to get to the off-licence he had no choice but to follow the same path, so he walked down into the shadowy, urine-stained recesses of the underpass once again, his head turning at every sound.

Despite feeling tense, jumpy, and jittery all the way through, he made it out of the underpass unapproached, and so now turned his attention to the bigger task at hand: stealing the alcohol. The bright lights of the shop sign beckoned him from over in the distance, and as he crossed the road towards the store he braced himself for action.

The plan went as well as it could have. He picked up the drink, headed for the tills, then, at the last minute, as the shopkeeper had been occupied with another customer, he'd drifted over to the door and slipped out without paying. He'd made it a safe distance away by the time the angry shop owner had come running out the front of the store, and despite his angry yells and fist waving he hadn't even bothered chasing after him.

The job was done but he knew that he had to keep on moving, so with a hand on each side of the crate he retraced his steps back towards his friend's squat where thirsty mouths needed watering.

Knowing that he now had another good few hours of drinking ahead of him, as well as having the comforting knowledge that it'd be another couple of days before the next theft was expected of him, he was in high spirits. But this all changed as he passed under the flyover for the second time, for as he stepped through the damp shadows he felt a steely grip clamp around his throat. He was thrown back against one of the concrete pillars and the entire case of beer fell from his hands, cans bursting and fizzing-up all over the pavement.

'What are you doing? Get off me you f—'

'I'm disappointed, Stanley. I really am.'

'You freak! Get your hand off my neck!'

He lashed out at the man but his lean build was deceiving, his strength unfaltering and relentless.

'You've had so many chances, so many opportunities.'

'I haven't got time for any more of your ramblings! Get...' Stanley paused, as if noticing something. 'Hey! How do you know my name? Who are you?'

He squinted, trying desperately to see who was inside the shadowy pit of the hood, but could see nothing except the faint bridge of the man's nose.

'I know more about you than you know about yourself.'

'If you want the beers just take them,' spat Stanley.

A gruff noise emanated from within the hood.

'Huh. So I can proceed to become you?

Drinking away my life and wasting away my days? If only I had the chance...'

Movement caught Stanley's eye from across the road as a man walked by. He panicked, thinking for a moment that it may have been the shopkeeper, but it wasn't him. He did, however, look vaguely familiar, and for a good few seconds Stanley couldn't pull his eyes away from this passing pedestrian despite the hooded vagrant continuing to rough him up.

'Are you listening to me?' raged the tramp. 'I said, if only I had the chance!'

'What do you want?' said Stanley, turning his head back towards him.

'I wanted to see you turn yourself around, to realise what potential you've got, to realise your amazing luck and good fortune. I wanted to see you achieve something; something that would've alleviated my own pain and torment.'

'You're bloody loopy! Get off of me!'

He was just about to raise a knee to the man's groin and shake himself free when another pedestrian came walking by, this time a woman on the same side of the road. Just a few feet away, she turned her head mockingly towards him, and once again Stanley saw something remarkably familiar in this stranger's features. The curve of her nose, the width of her chin, the cheek bones...

'But it's too late now, you've blown it!' the attacker continued.

'Look, what is this?'

There was a stony silence for a few seconds, during which Stanley could only lean back against the pillar and look helplessly towards the faint outline of a face before him.

'Did you know that the amount of sperm cells a man creates over the course of a lifetime adds up literally to the hundreds of *billions*?'

'What?'

'On the night of your conception alone,' continued the man, 'you were in competition with up to one billion other sperm cells. That's one billion potential lives—'

'What are you? Are you a junkie, or some kind of preacher?'

'...one billion potential lives, people who could've become artists, scientists, doctors, engineers, astronauts or writers.' The hood leaned in closer, so close that Stanley could now see two thin, glistening eyes staring out at him. 'But you know what, Stanley? Those people didn't make it into existence. You beat them here; you took the life that they were all competing for. So tell me: what exactly have you done with it?'

The man was now so close to him that the mist of his breath was merging with his, and the wide brim of his hood was touching his forehead.

'I don't have to explain myself to you! Get the fuck off me! Who do you think you are?'

It was then, whilst maintaining an iron grip on his neck, that the man pulled back his baggy hood and revealed himself. For Stanley, it was like looking in the mirror.

'I'm one of the many who didn't make it, Stanley. One of the many who was beaten before life even began, one of the many who could've grown into something great, something legendary.'

Stunned into a paralysing silence, Stanley could do nothing but study the man's face. His prominent nose, pointed ears, crooked teeth and dishevelled hair gave such a strong resemblance to his own, it looked like the man had stolen his own features. Looking at this replica of himself he wondered whether he might've simply bumped into a long-lost brother, or a troubled relative who'd tracked him down online. The tingling feeling in his gut, however, was telling him a different story.

The two of them were now causing a scene, and clusters of passers-by were stopping to see what the commotion was. With the damaged beer cans rolling and leaking by his feet Stanley was reminded that he was still too close to the off-licence for comfort, and so made a fresh attempt to shake himself free and scarper.

'Enough of this shit!' he shouted, straining and turning against the hand on his neck. 'If you want to rant and ramble on all night, crawl back to your cardboard box and rant to yourself, because I haven't got time for it!'

A wry grin formed across the man's face, causing his eyes and teeth to glisten from the glow of a distant streetlight.

'Fine, I'll let you go, but it's not just me you have to answer to.' With one last surge of strength, the man yanked his collar and brought his face even closer. 'Like I said, there was one billion people who never made it.'

Pushed aside and now free from the man's grip, Stanley straightened himself and edged away from him. Most of the beers were ruined so he didn't even bother picking up the crate, instead he began to turn and head back to the squat empty handed. But what he saw all around him stopped him in his tracks, causing him to pause in disbelief. The pockets of people across the road had grown in number, and were now all staring unashamedly at him. And there were more approaching, too, from both sides of the road. Figures were appearing all around him, lining the pavements, stood on the road crossings, and drifting across the patches of grass in the middle-distance. Eyes peered out from behind bus stops, heads turned in passing cars, ashen faces looked up from wooden benches, and up above the flyover rows of onlookers were leaning over the rail casting their hateful, fiery glances down towards where he stood. But it wasn't just the vast numbers that scared him, it was the faces themselves, the similar, replicated, homogeneous faces that all looked related, regardless of whether they were male or female.

As the crowds continued to advance he slowly retreated, and the hooded man finally called out his parting words.

'Don't ever say you didn't have a chance.'

As these grave words were sinking in, a deep murmur echoed through the streets, an ominous growl that spoke of an impending doom. This low, rumbling, earthy noise made the tarmac underneath his feet vibrate, causing his balance to falter. It was then that he saw movement on the horizon, a giant slither flowing down the curve of the main road. A flux of bodies, a gargantuan crowd, all advancing down towards him like a billion-strong army with hearts full of rage.

His casual retreat turned into an all-out sprint in the opposite direction as the behemoth mob came towards him, a human tidal wave consuming the nighttime streets. The thunder and roar grew louder and louder, however, no matter how fast he ran, and before long he began to feel the brush of hands against his coat sleeves, and sharp tugs at his collar. An endless stream of silhouettes emerged from every surrounding side street and alleyway; more yells, more tugs, more screams from over his shoulder, then a swiping kick to his ankle sent him stumbling and staggering to the curbside. A futile attempt was made to shield himself from the onslaught of kicks and punches raining down from above, but with too many fists to count let alone defend himself from he resorted to curling up into a ball, regressing back into the fetal position as the life he'd been granted came to a harsh, painful end.

VOYAGER

In 1977 NASA built and launched two space probes. Each probe has a golden record attached to its exterior containing sound recordings, codes, messages, and a map—all designed to help any extraterrestrial life form to find planet Earth.

Both probes have left the solar system, and are now flying through deep space.

They found a golden record, and followed what it said
And after they arrived, the land was awash with red
The trick was deceiving, an irresistible smell
It pulled them all towards it, and then they dropped and fell

PART ONE

I'm standing by the end of the hospital bed as the police officer fires away questions from behind his big rubber mask. I'm wearing a mask, too. We all are, in fact: the police officer, the doctor, me, and the angry-looking man by the window. The only person in the room who isn't wearing a mask is the woman lying on the bed. There's no point in her wearing one now, and even if there were, a mask wouldn't fit over her swollen cheeks anyway.

'Just start from the beginning,' the doctor says, noticing that the woman is having trouble answering the questions. 'Tell the officer everything that you told me.'

The woman nods her head in agreement, or at least I think she does. It's hard to tell with all the puffiness.

'L...Like I said, I was walking my dog through the park. I'd decided to...to take a slightly different route than the one I usually take as...as I had no other plans for the morning and had some time to kill. I headed up the hill just a few hundred metres in from the entrance gate and...and I strolled up through the woodlands. I knew that there was a narrow dirt path that ran all the way through the trees and back to the main field, sho I thought I'd try it out and go that way.'

Every now and then the woman's speech becomes slurred, and words come out of her rubbery lips mispronounced. Everybody acts like they don't notice, though.

'Was there anyone else around at this point?' asks the officer, looming over the bed with his tall, crane-like frame.

'There were...There were a few other people in the field, but I was alone once I was in among-shhd the trees.'

I can see her through the plastic eye-piece of my mask as she begins to sob uncontrollably, prompting her husband to move away from the window and take her bare hand into his gloved hand. During this uncomfortable pause I try to picture the exact area in the park that she's talking about, and I'm fairly sure I know it. Being the park warden, I know pretty much every square foot of the place, and this pathway that she mentioned is part of my daily patrol.

After her bout of tears subsides she spends a painful minute trying to dab her eyes with some tissue. Her skin looks sore and sensitive, and in addition to this, her eyes are half-submerged in the rippling, inflated folds of her upper and lower lids. Eventually, after much painful fumbling, she's able to continue:

'F...Fred was way up ahead of me. A...About two hundred yards further up.'

'Fred is...er, *was* your dog, right?' the officer interrupted.

'Yeshh,' sobbed the woman. 'He...He looked like he could see something, or maybe smell something further up the path that was driving him crazy. He was off the lead and running wild so I began to chase after him, shouting and calling ashh I climbed the hill.'

'And then what happened?' asks the officer, his voice sounding echoey behind the mask.

'It...It washh then that the smell hit me.'

Despite the monstrous folds engorging her face, we can all see her expression change as she utters the word "smell". Looking down at her now, it's clear that she's recalling some deeply profound sensation.

'It was just so...beautiful. It was like running into a cloud of perfume. I'd never smelt anything like that before. As soon as I caught that scent, I couldn't help but run further towardsh it.'

'What did it smell like?' asks the officer, his echoey voice laced with morbid curiosity.

'It smelt like...like...*ecstasy*.'

Her arms wrap around herself as she describes this smell, and as she lies there, incapacitated on the bed, she reminds me of a junkie going cold turkey, a life-long addict craving another hit of their preferred poison. The room is dead silent apart from the wheezing sounds of her nostrils as she sniffs through the narrowed passages, apparently trying to summon up some last traces of this seductive aroma.

'And then what happened?' prompts the officer, the woman's junkie-like behaviour clearly making him uncomfortable.

'I...I just wanted to get closer to that smell. Nothing else mattered. I just wanted to take in as much of it as I could, sho I carried on running up the hill towards the trees where it was coming from. For a while I was so caught up in the scent that I forgot all about Fred, but then, further into the trees...I shaw him!'

The woman's bloated form trembles with agony and torment as she recollects a mental image, so much so that the doctor actually begins to step forward to help. Before he gets to the bed, however, she regains a certain amount of composure and carries on:

'He was caught up in these horrible vines. These black vines, they were...they were curled around his little body like snakes trying to strangle him. It was everywhere. Everything up there was covered in vines or this...this black moss. It was growing around tree trunks, hanging from branches...even the ground itself was like a black carpet covered with this growth.'

'So it was this moss that your dog was caught up in?' asked the officer.

'The vines had him! He was caught up in the wiry vines! At first I couldn't shee him, I could only hear him. This horrible howling that I'd never heard come out of him before. I followed the sound further and further into the trees, fighting through this growth that was all around me. It was growing so quickly that I could literally see it shpread before my eyes! As...As soon as I got to him I knew that it was too late. His little body was...it was nothing but a tangle of fur caught up in these vicious-looking vines, curling tighter and tighter.'

'How far into these vines were you?'

'Oh, I don't know...fifty yards or so. It felt dreamy and disoriented in there, what with that thick smell hanging in the air. It was like I was being consumed by the forest somehow, my will to survive weakening by the second. But...But something snapped me out of it and made me come to. I panicked and pulled myself away from it all, the sharp tugging vines and the smell, heading back out towards the open field.'

'I think that's enough now, officer,' says the husband. 'She needs to rest.' He looks over towards the doctor to see if he'll back him up, and sure enough, the doctor nods in agreement.

The officer makes a couple more notes in his pad then turns towards the door, beckoning me to follow. Outside in the corridor, we both take off our masks.

'Do you know the area that she was referring to?' he asks me.

'Yes, I know it,' I reply. 'It's over on the eastern side of the park.'

'I'm going to need you to show me where it is. I'll drive us over there right after I get the place cordoned off.'

I stand there idly for a moment as he takes out his phone and barks orders to someone on the other end of the line. Once the message is put across that the park needs to be closed off to the public, we exit the hospital and climb into the squad car parked outside.

△△△

A group of officers are already at the park when we arrive. They're standing outside the main entrance gate, moving dog-walkers and pedestrians along. They give a brief nod as we pull up to the curb, then lead us towards their van which has a selection of protective equipment laid out in the back of it. Five minutes later I feel like an extra in some B-grade sci-fi movie, kitted out to the nines in paper overalls, boots, gloves, and of course my mask, which I had already.

The two of us make our way across the field, our heavy boots raking up clods of mud and dirt along the way. Our communication is stifled due to the cumbersome rubber masks clamped over our faces, but if we shout loud enough we can hear each other. It takes around ten minutes to reach the hill that the woman described, and as soon as it comes into view I can tell straight away that the trees and foliage at the top of it has changed. Things look altered, different; the leaves and bushes look denser than they usually do, the branches darker and slicker. I turn my masked head towards the officer to get his attention. 'This is it.'

'Up there? In those trees?'

'Yes. Those are the trees that the woman described.'

We both follow the muddy pathway towards the towering trees up above, but now I'm at the back, following the officer's lead. Peering up at the sinister-looking tangle of forest fifty feet ahead of us, I raise no objections to letting him go first, feeling more than happy for him to be the first one to venture into the dark greenery. Our boots squelch with every step, and the mud has now darkened to a sickly shade of black, the texture noticeably different even under the heavy industrial rubber soles that cover my feet.

As we walk under a canopy and into the main patch of forest, terror strikes my very core. I'm surrounded by strangled tree-trunks, thick barks wrapped tightly in wiry strands of ivy. The thorny arms snake and spiral upwards, suffocating the beech and pine trees with no mercy.

'What the hell *is* this?' gasps the officer, looking around nervously at this murderous organism.

'It's clearly some kind of weed,' I reply, talking from my years of experience working in parks
and gardens, 'but I've never seen it before.'

'Well, we need to keep on going until we find this dog. I need something to confirm the woman's story.'

We venture further in, although neither of us really wants to. The weed seems to writhe and grow angrier right before our eyes, and I find myself wondering whether the ecstatic scent that the woman described is present beyond the tight seal of my mask.

It doesn't take long to find the dog. It's pearly-white tufts of hair protrude from the knots of black ivy in wispy, wavy strands, drawing our eyes towards its dead limbs that dangle limply. The animal is little more than a twisted ball of fur suspended three feet above the ground by the ravenous arms that encircle it, the life literally drained out of its veins and arteries.

'We need to get out of here,' I say.

'I just need to take a picture of the damn thing,' replies the officer, fumbling around for his camera.

A series of flashes burst out of the digital camera as the officer snaps away, and every one of them illuminates the carcass of the dog just long enough for me to see extra details that I don't really want to see: long thorns sunk deep into the pink skin, thick red tendrils of coagulated blood drooping down from the matted fur, protruding bones disjointed under the immense pressure of the black stringy vines.

'OK, let's go,' shouts the officer, switching off his camera once the last picture is taken.

We retrace our steps down the path, scrambling back towards the open field. The black moss on the ground has thickened even more now, resembling a deep blanket laid out over the bumpy contours of the terrain. The canopy in which we entered looks smaller now, and the circle of daylight up ahead is literally shrinking as the weeds proliferate. We're running now, charging towards the closing gap before we get sealed into this thorny den of death. I feel the sickly grip of ivy spikes tugging on my paper overalls, but we make it back out to the open hilltop in one piece, the bright field stretched out in front of us.

'Don't take your mask off,' the officer yells, as we make it back out to relative safety.

I had no plans to do so. There's no doubt in my mind that that smell is hanging thick in the air around us, ready to lure us back to our deaths. I do, however, look back. I look back up towards the slope, up towards the thicket of trees from which we've just escaped. The trees looked different as soon as we entered the park, but now they look completely unrecognisable.

All I can see now at the summit of the slope is a growing ball of heavy black fuzz, smothering and consuming everything underneath it, spiky tips reaching up into the air like sharp fingernails scratching at the sky.

'What's that?'

When I hear the officer's voice from over my shoulder I presume that he's referring to the black growth up on the hill, but when I turn to look at him he's pointing down to a mound of dirt a few feet away from us. From where I'm standing it looks like the work of a fox, or a mole, maybe, but judging by the look on the officer's face he's obviously come to a different conclusion.

'What's what?'

'There's something in there. Down in that hole.'

We walk over to it and take a look, and sure enough, sitting there in the chewed up soil, there's a metallic, spherical object. It's gold and shiny, and about twelve inches in diameter.

'It looks like a golden record,' says the officer, crouching down to pick it up.

I watch him pick it up out of the dirt, and it is indeed some kind of record, rather like the old vinyl records that people used to play music on back in the day. Something about it looks familiar, and I lean in to get a closer look.

'What are those inscriptions?' I ask.

Using his thick rubber glove, the officer

wipes some of the muck off of the disc, revealing a set of diagrams etched into it. As soon as I see them more clearly I immediately know what I'm looking at, but I don't quite believe it, not for one second. My initial thought is that it must be some kind of joke or prank, some prop that someone left here after a drunken night out or something. But then I remember that I'm dressed in heavy protective clothing with an unknown organism raging away behind me, and I'm forced to at least consider the notion that's spinning around in my head. The officer notices the stunned look on my face, and asks me what's wrong.

'This can't be true,' I reply. 'It just can't be.'

'Do you know what this is?'

'Y...Yes, I think so.'

I'm convinced that the object the officer is holding in his hands is the Voyager Record, or one of them at least. I remember seeing pictures of them as a kid, and reading about them in some science magazine. They were sent up into space by NASA back in the late seventies as time capsules, displaying information about planet Earth—and the humans living here.

'Well, what is it?' pressed the officer.

I tell him. Feeling ridiculous as I do so.

'Is that what these markings are? Information about life on Earth?' he asks, running his finger along the elaborate drawings and diagrams.

'Yes, and also...'

'Also what?'

'Also directions on how to get here,' I mumble, as nausea begins to consume me.

A tense silence ensues between us as we both ponder the implications of what we've just found. Under normal circumstances it'd be laughable to suggest that this thing was actually one of the original Voyager Records, but with this menacing weed thriving and expanding behind us on the hill, it doesn't actually seem that far-fetched.

'Let's get back to the car,' says the officer, who, by this point, has given up trying to look brave and authoritative.

We literally sprint back to the park entrance gate, the Voyager Record dangling from the officer's gloved hand like a plastic frisbee. More squad cars have arrived by the time we get there, and I'm swiftly stripped of my protective gear and ushered into the back of one.

I spend the rest of the afternoon at the station answering questions. There are no accusations against me, no charges or fines, they simply want to gauge what I know about this strange golden disc. There's a nervousness about most of the officers in the constabulary, a sense that everybody is way out of their depth, and it makes me jittery and full of apprehension. They are completely unprepared for this bizarre situation that has fallen upon them, but I have sympathy for them.

My words, for what they're worth, are both tape recorded and written down in a book. By six o' clock I'm free to return home to my apartment.

PART TWO

It's been two weeks since I saw that thing in the park, but the whole fiasco is far from over. I got a phone call the next day from my employer, telling me that my work duties are suspended for the foreseeable future.

I've been occupying myself with odd jobs around the flat, taking long walks, reading, trying to keep myself distracted from the countless questions circling around in my head. But it's no use, I know that what I saw that day was not terrestrial, not from this world. Every time I close my eyes I see the woman's dog, I see that twisted little ball of white fur hanging dead in the ivy, puncture marks dotting its skin. The police politely—but firmly—told me not to speak to anyone about the incident, and that only makes it all worse. With no one to speak to about it the images and pictures grow and swirl unmarshalled around my mind, taking on new forms and making me question my own sanity and validity.

While I was out on one of my walks a few days ago, I took a deliberate detour that took me along a road that runs adjacent to the park entrance. I couldn't help it, I just had to go and see what was going on there, to gauge the current situation. Uniformed officers were still present outside the park gates, maintaining a tight cordon, speaking to pockets of concerned locals who were loitering around and trying to work out what was happening—or at least, this is what I thought they were doing at the time.

When I first saw these small crowds of local residents milling about along the road, I naturally came to the conclusion that they were there to speak to the police, but that conclusion has since altered. Things changed on my return home that day. Walking back through the surrounding streets and alleyways, with the park grounds still in the close vicinity, a faint scent drifted through the air that teased and tantalised every cell in my body. The sensation was very brief and transient, lasting less than a second, but I felt it strongly. The aroma floated up through my nostrils and it was more glorious, more divine, more orgasmic even, than anything else my olfactory senses had ever experienced before. No word or sentence could ever describe how good it was, nor could it describe the sheer amount of willpower and self control it took to restrain myself from trying to get closer to it. The gentle breeze that was present that afternoon helped, I suppose, carrying the smell away just as quickly as it had delivered it, but it still took an enormous amount of effort for me to control myself.

After this intense experience had passed my thoughts returned to the local people standing around outside the park, along with a dark suspicion that they were all becoming hooked on this scent.

Flashbacks of the sick woman on the hospital bed have been plaguing me since this happened, flashbacks of looking down at her thin arms cradled across her chest, her quivering body in a state of withdrawal. It seemed crazy to me at the time, pathetic even, but now, after experiencing that fragrance for just a fleeting moment, I have to grudgingly admit to myself that I understand.

△△△

The last few evenings have been frustrating. I haven't been out much, instead I've been scouring the local news stations on the radio trying to see whether anyone's reporting on the incident at the park, but I haven't found a single thing. The TV stations are the same, not a single mention. It's as if someone's trying to cover the whole thing up—either that, or they're simply in denial about what's going on.

But this secrecy or denial cannot continue for very long, because I know that that thing is still out there. If I look outside my bathroom window, out of the small pane of glass above the cistern, I'm looking east, in the direction of the park. It's awkward and uncomfortable, and I have to crane my neck slightly to see the right place, but if I get myself in the right position it's possible for me to see the park from my little window. Some of the grounds are hidden and obscured behind the various rooftops and buildings, but I can see most of it. And this view outside my bathroom window, this miniature tableau, has altered over the course of the last week. A dark blot has appeared above the line of rooftops over in the distance, a black smudge that has been rising steadily over the chimneys and tiles. Surely I can't be the only person monitoring this visual deformity, this rising shadow expanding over the town?

△△△

I'm staring out of the narrow window in my bathroom again, but now there are small dark specks dashing across the sky. These tiny specks, these curious little black smudges hurtling across the air, are small birds flying frantically towards the park, plummeting towards their deaths. I'm wearing a makeshift mask as I watch this suicidal, kamikaze act, because I no longer consider the air outside safe to breath.

It seems as though nothing is immune from that deceptive odour emanating from the monstrous growth on the horizon, not even birds. I've lost count of how many I've seen darting across the sky now, sailing towards their demise. I'm not totally sure how other animals are reacting to what's going on, but I have noticed that the foxes and cats that usually scratch and rummage around my apartment's communal bin area are no longer there.

My decision to start wearing a mask at home came about the other morning when I found myself crouching by the front door on my hands and knees. I was half asleep, dazed, with no recollection of even having gotten out of bed. Naked and dishevelled, bleary and delirious, I was clumsily trying to suck in air through the gaps around the door frame, pulling down on the handle that thankfully was locked. At some point during the night that scent had drifted into my apartment block and worked its way up the stairwell, trying its best to seep into my flat. Luckily something woke me up before I could manage to open the door and drag myself outside in full view of the neighbours. I don't know what it was, but something brought me back to my senses. But the scariest part of all of this is that I actually didn't need to worry about being seen by anyone. As far as I can tell, from wandering around the many floors of this building since, the place is completely deserted. All the residents have gone, vanished, and I seem to be the only one left. Exactly when this mini exodus occurred is beyond me, but it certainly occurred at some point because there's nobody else here.

Another bird sails past in the distance and I pull myself away from the bathroom window, deciding that I've had enough and that I need to take some kind of action. It's been days since I've ventured out onto the streets, days since I've left the confines of this abandoned block of flats, and I can't stay locked up in here for ever. With the mask still wrapped around my face I clamber around the flat, looking for my wallet, phone and keys. Stuffing them all into my pockets, I hastily leave before I change my mind and lose my bravado.

The streets outside seem just as deserted as my apartment block, and I'm all alone as I traipse along the pavement with a roughly-cut piece of fabric wrapped around my face. Every shop that I pass is empty, every office complex quiet and inactive, and every now and again I come across a house with its front door left wide open. Naturally, I head in the general direction of the park. The silence ringing through the empty streets is eerie and unsettling, but as I cover some distance and get closer to the park grounds a low murmur becomes noticeable to me. It feels like a dim vibration at first, a low humming noise, but it steadily rises in volume as I keep on walking, growing sharper and more distinct as I navigate my way through the avenues, lanes and intersections. After another five minutes or so the odd person starts to appear here and there, desperate-looking faces emerging from lanes and alleyways. Everyone I see looks dazed and bewildered, but they all walk with purpose and speed, heading in one direction. No one's speaking to each other or looking in each other's direction, they're just putting one foot in front of the other, following their noses like sleepwalking cattle.

Turning a corner, I finally reach the entrance gates to the park. The whole road is swarming with people, heaving from curb to curb with shuffling bodies. There are a couple of police cars present, but no officers in sight. The humming noise is loud and clear now amongst the dimwitted crowd, and I now recognise it to be the undiluted craving sounds of hundreds of sick, disturbed addicts. The sound is a chorus of guttural moans and groans resonating through the dank air, a symphony of undignified gasping and panting.

There's a huge struggle to get through the entrance gates and I'm unwillingly caught up in the flow, arms and elbows digging into me as I get dragged along. During this struggle, the unspeakable happens. Someone tries to pull me back and overtake me, their hand tugging me from behind. They lose their grip on my shoulder and start clawing at my clothing instead, and then, with one swift, whipping motion, my mask is pulled away from my face and chucked to the ground. Within seconds it's trampled upon by dozens of feet and then kicked away somewhere, leaving me with no protection against the tang in the air other than the sleeve of my shirt. I try my best to keep my face buried in the crease of my arm, but the attempt is futile. Someone steps on my toes and elbows me in the ribs simultaneously, sending me flying into the park's big iron railings. Both of my arms are needed to soften and cushion the impact, and I inadvertently end up taking in a generous lungful of contaminated air. It rushes towards my nose and mouth like compressed gas shooting out of a canister, and I feel it sticking to the narrow passageways of my sinuses. And instantly, just like that, I become one of *them*. All of my fight and resistance crumbles away at the first touch of this potent scent, my very will to survive and make it out of this calamity evaporating into nothing. All of a sudden, after taking this first breath, there's only one thing that matters to me: getting more.

The thing is, I'm completely aware of what's happening, completely aware of what I'm doing, but that doesn't stop me. I know that I'm now on a suicide walk into the grounds of the park, a one-way mission to inhale a scent that'll take me closer to a viscous, hungry organism that'll most likely kill me, but I can't stop myself because the smell is just *so good*. It's succulent, it's divine, and every breath that I take makes me more addicted and hooked on it.

The big field that me and the officer walked across has now completely transformed. The ground is completely black, with numerous shapes and forms embedded in it. Tiny carcasses crunch and squelch under my feet as I step across this vast feeding ground, the countless mice, rats, cats, dogs, squirrels and foxes rotting and mummifying all around me. There are dozens of us walking across the field, everyone carelessly treading on dry, bloodless corpses as we head towards the big hill up ahead. The hill itself is a sight to behold. It's like an organic skyscraper, thorns and leaves reaching up towards the clouds like they're trying to pluck the fluffy white shapes out of the air. As well as this, thick trunks of ivy have snaked their way down the hill, covering the long slope like giant cables. The shapes embedded in the ground get bigger and bigger as I reach the foot of the hill, and there's a sickening moment when I realise that I'm walking across human remains, long femurs and shoulder blades crunching under my weight like dry twigs. The revulsion of it all gets worse as I ascend further up the hill, however, for the bodies seem to be fresher, and squelching noises accompany the snapping and crunching. Wet skin glistens beneath me whenever I dare to look down, fresh puncture marks oozing pus and claret.

But even this orgy of decay is not enough to deter me from pursuing more and more of this scent, such is its delectability and charm. This horror reaches me through a distorted lens, a lens of addiction that dulls my senses and puts my survival instinct of standby. On and on I trudge, somehow managing to avoid the writhing strands trying their best to wrap themselves around my ankles. I'm sucking in huge breaths through my mouth and nose as I go, every inhalation making my body tingle with pleasure from the hairs on my head all the way down to the soles of my feet. The odour has permeated through to my very core, invaded my cells, become a part of my very being. I simply have to get closer to the main source of it all, up to where the aroma is at its strongest and most potent. A small part of me, the part that is still capable of thinking clearly, knows that I'm heading towards my very demise, but its influence on my actions is nothing compared the ravenous beast growing on the hill.

ΔΔΔ

The sky is darkening, dropping down to a warm amber. I've been looking up at it for what seems like hours now, staring up through the mesh of limbs that encircle my vision. I'm one of them; another lump in the field, another bag of bones to be trampled over, another weeping bag of pus and blood, another defeated junkie consumed by the growth. Life is slipping away from me, my blood leaking into the dark vines, but somehow my brain still functions. I'm alert and conscious enough to speculate on what's going on around me, watching the horrifying events unfold as I sink further down into this mass feeding ground.

A thundering clap erupts above me, directly overhead. A dark spot then appears in the sky, descending and growing larger. Everything seems to shake and vibrate, the carpet of flesh, bones and ivy grinding against itself under the pressure. The vibrating pressure intensifies as this spherical object comes down, hovering and lingering over the long trunks of ivy. It's studying the landscape, gauging the results of its experiment, assessing the current state of the land.

This craft, this capsule, agitates the ivy and a fresh jolt of pain runs through me as the thorns squeeze and twist tighter into my skin. Whoever, or whatever, is up there in that vessel wants to be alone in the universe, free from threat and competition. If they wanted to use us in any way they would've kept us alive and well, fit enough to work for them, but instead they've exterminated us in the cruelest way possible. They're here to exterminate the life that threatens their own existence, to wipe out their cosmological neighbours before they get a chance to become too smart or too developed. It dawns on me now that the ivy was planted here to do the dirty work for them, to evaluate the strength of the evolved life forms that inhabit this fertile planet.

It's moving again now, moving away across the simmering horizon. I watch it leave, whilst tangled here in the arms of death. Its smooth body skims through the air, graceful and elegant, as fine dust sprinkles out from behind it, forming faint, descending contrails. Long puffy clouds of seeds and spores fill the sky behind the craft, drifting along in the light breeze, ready to drop down and impregnate more soil. This grainy haze, this organic mist, is the last thing I ever see.

FOOD FOR THOUGHT

MUSINGS ON HUMAN EXISTENCE

A baby's thrown into this world of chance
Another life, another living branch
Rolled into the hardy game of life
No choice, no say, a random toss of dice

For every man alive, there was a million
Who lost the race and sank into oblivion
But did they really lose by not existing?
Being spared of all life's ills and heavy lifting?

Trapped inside the ruthless realm of time
And stuck inside a rotting human mind
One has to ask the question, time to time
Is life a gift, or just an awful grind?

DAMNED BY FORTUNE

There was a lonesome man, well in his senior years

His mind was an awful mess, and his eyes full of tears

He wanted to find some cash, to make his bank funds grow

But there was a nasty catch, of which he didn't know

'OK, Arthur, it's time for your shot,' calls the woman from out in the living room.

I was in the middle of getting dressed when I heard her, shuffling around my bedroom trying to remember where everything was.

'I'll just be a second,' I reply, feeling more than a little disorientated.

The voice bellowing out from the living room belongs to Mrs Clark, my personal nurse. I'm always grateful for her company and I often wonder what I'd do if she weren't here everyday, checking up on me. Living with an undiagnosed illness is hard, especially when you have no one else for support.

With a mish-mash of creased clothes hanging off of me I trot feebly through the hallway where I finally see her sitting there on my sofa, her hair pinned tightly back in its usual style as she prepares the syringe. I'm not sure what concoction's floating in the barrel of the needle today, as I've long given up trying to memorise the long medicinal names; all I know is that it's good for my condition. Sitting next to her on the sofa, I roll up my sleeve and let her swap my arm with a cotton bud.

'How are you feeling today, Arthur?' she asks, looking over at me.

Feeling slightly embarrassed, I tell her the truth. I tell her that yesterday is fuzzy, and the day before that is a complete blur. I try to avoid being so blunt and honest because it makes all of her hard work look as though it's in vain, but it's the truth. I remember very little from day to day.

'Just relax for me, this won't take a second,' she says, holding my arm in her lap.

A slight pain swells up in my arm as the clear solution is injected into it, but I'm used to it now. With the injection out of the way, Mrs Clark turns to me and says, 'Are you ready for your mental exercises?'

'I sure am,' I reply, although I say this mainly out of politeness. My medication is already making my head spin, so I feel far from ready, but I don't like to disappoint her. She pulls a laptop out of her bag and puts it down on the coffee table, loading it up. A sick feeling rises up in my stomach as the bright screen comes to life, and I struggle to keep my concentration and focus. I suppose the exercises aren't that strenuous. They consist of a little hand-to-eye coordination game and some reading and number games, among other things, but they just never really seem to get any easier.

By the time the first exercise has loaded up I can hardly focus on the screen. It appears before me as a swirling fluorescent sun, blurry with no discernible edges. I don't mention this to Mrs

Clark though, of course, I simply put on a brave face.

'OK, when you're ready, raise your right index finger up above your head, then, with your fingertip, try to touch the small circle on the screen.'

Following her instructions, I raise my arm high up in the air and then lower it forwards towards the screen, aiming for the faint circle that I think she's referring to. It takes me several attempts to get it right, but I get there in the end, and I activate the next level of the program. I'm then faced with the reading exercise. This is often the hardest one of all because I have to try and focus on small printed words, but I try my best, and read out the sentences that come up on the screen. I seem to do quite well, and Mrs Clark applauds my effort, guiding me along to the next level of the program which is the retinal examination. This is definitely the easiest part. All I have to do is stare closely at two oval shapes on the screen while they examine my eyes. I have no idea how this technology works but it sure is impressive, and I stare at the screen patiently while it does its thing.

A few moments pass and then a green light appears, signalling the end of the exercises and tests. Mrs Clark spends another few minutes tapping buttons, typing in numbers and digits, but I simply flop back against the sofa, giving in to the strong, nauseating effects of the medication.

My old life is mostly lost to me, apart from a few hazy memories and recollections here and there. I never used to have the problems that I have today, I used to be healthy, but things changed a few years back when I fainted during an afternoon stroll. It happened by an underpass about two miles away from my home, and I was rushed off in an ambulance. Thankfully, I was given the help that I needed, and I was soon granted regular visits by the delightful Mrs Clark, for whom nothing is too much trouble. I tell you, if I ever make a full recovery, it'll be down to the amazing work that she has done for me.

△△△

With my meds and exercises taken care of and Mrs Clark gone, I feel so dizzy and drained that I feel like taking a nap. When I walk back into my bedroom, however, I see a scrap of paper sitting on top of my dresser. It's a note that I've left myself, which I often do, and when I read it its contents all come flooding back to me. Of course! I was planning a little trip through town today, and I wrote this note yesterday to remind myself. An address and phone number is written on the bottom of the page, along with two words: *Time Machine*. I suppose I should really explain this. You see, the most bizarre thing happened to me yesterday. I was digging through some of the old boxes in my spare room, trying to sort out the junk from the valuables, when I found a stack of old newspapers. There were about twenty of them, all stuffed into a tattered box covered in dust. Of course, I ended up reading through some of them, scanning the yellowed pages and headlines out of boredom. Anyway, I found an advert that caught my eye. It was a small, private advert buried in amongst the countless "want ads" and "lonely hearts" pages, but something about it immediately caught my attention. It was printed in an unusual, italic font, and it was also enticing in its lack of details. Some of the words were barely decipherable due to the age of the thin paper, but most were readable:

Machine for hire

Ready to take you back to

your missed opportunities.

Affordable rates.

Call 0945 366 072 for

more details

A few things ran through my mind when I

first saw this advert. At first I thought it might be a joke of some kind, a couple of pranksters putting it in the paper just to see who'd be stupid enough to actually call the number. Then I considered the possibility of it being a scam. I thought it could've been one of those rigged phone numbers that lock you into a huge bill as soon as your connected to it, fleecing you of your hard-earned cash. I eventually put the paper aside and began occupying myself with other things around the house, but it'd intrigued me to the point where I simply had to return to it and dial the number. Taking an insane punt, a ridiculous long shot, I actually tried calling it. Sure, I knew that it might've been a scam, but I don't really have any money to lose anyway, so what was the harm in trying?

But, to my amazement, it was neither a scam nor a joke—at least I don't think it was. A man answered after a few rings, his voice calm and sage-like. He didn't sound like a prankster or a scammer, so I made a couple of serious inquiries about the machine. I asked him what it was, and where it was kept, but I only got an answer to one of the questions. He'd been quite vague and distant about the true nature of the machine he was advertising, but he was quick to give me its location nonetheless, so I at least ended the call armed with something.

So this is what my little trip across town is for: to take a look at this mysterious machine.

Clearly, I have my own idea about what it could be, but I can't know for sure until I see it in the flesh. Gathering up my keys, phone and wallet, I get ready to leave the house. This is no easy task by the way, because I'm still feeling the effects of my jab, but I push myself through it out of a desire to see what this thing really is. Stumbling out of my front door, squinting against the dazzling sunlight, I feel a little guilty towards Mrs Clark, who usually advises me not to venture outside too much. But today is different, today I have a special reason for going out, and if this machine really is what I think it is, I might somehow be able to repay dear Mrs Clark for her unceasing kindness.

So what do I want with a time machine anyway, I hear you ask? Why would I want to travel backwards or forwards through time? Well, the reason is simple: I'm unhappy. I'm desperately unhappy and I want to try and do something about it, try and change things. As lucky as I am to have the help of somebody like Mrs Clark and her team, I'm completely alone in life, alone and falling apart. If I can alter the course of history things will turn out differently, and I might not end up in this dire situation.

Remember I told you that I still have hazy memories and recollections from the past? Well, perhaps the most prominent memory of all is of a local man who stumbled upon a fortune a few years back. I've forgotten his name now, and to be honest I can't even remember what he looked like, but I remember clearly how he became rich. He found some old Roman coins whilst walking out in the meadows, and he dug them up and took them home with him. A couple of days later a reputable antiques dealer estimated their value to be in the six figure region, and he went on to sell them at an auction for something like £1.5 million. It was all over the local news, I remember that much. And if I really do get a chance to travel back in time, I'm going to travel back to about six months before those coins were discovered and tell my younger self where they are. I could then be the one who becomes rich, the one with plenty of money! Yes, I know it's morally questionable, I know that it could be considered to be outright wrong, but can you really blame me? And, also, before you start judging me, consider this: if I end up with a lot of money, the first thing I'm going to do is give Mrs Clark a massive paycheck for everything that she's done for me. Whether I end up getting ill again or not, I'll do that, you mark my words. And if you bear that in mind, it's not that much of a despicable act after all, is it?

So this is where I'm headed today, I'm going over to the address I was given to see if this device is the real deal or not. The journey gets off to a bad start. In my absentmindedness, I get on the wrong bus and end up going five miles in the wrong direction. It was quite a major delay, I must admit, but afterwards, after gathering my wits and getting my bearings again, I manage to navigate myself over to the right side of town and locate the address. Walking through a few residential streets, passing a number of houses and gardens, a double row of garages eventually appear at the end of a sleepy cul-de-sac.

I gingerly walk towards them, finding the silence of the surrounding streets unsettling. The garages look battered and unused, but I can see that one of them towards the back is open, its rusty steel door sticking out at a horizontal angle. Reaching the edge of this open lockup I peer inside, taking in the assortment of odds and ends stacked up against the walls. Everything is draped and covered with cloths so I don't really know what I'm looking at, but I study the shapes closely anyway.

'You must be Arthur.'

The voice makes me jump so much my feet nearly leave the ground. Movement stirs within the shadowy space, and a tall silhouette emerges from the boxes and the gloom. He advances towards me and extends a gloved hand. He has an anachronistic look about him. A wide-brimmed hat sits atop his head, and a long dark coat hangs from his shoulders.

'Come on inside, it's through here,' he says, and I follow him into the dim storage space.

A square, pointy object is sat in the corner, and he grabs a piece of its cover and gives it a tug. I'm then confronted with something that resembles an old passport photo booth, something that wouldn't look out of place in a train station or a post office.

'So...what is it?' I ask.

'You know exactly what it is,' replies the man, his incredulous, deep-set eyes staring at me from under the dark brim of his hat.

A cynical side of me takes over and I look around, half expecting to be the butt of some hidden camera practical joke.

'But...'

'Look, I don't blame you for being dubious, but it works, trust me.'

I was still hesitant, and it showed.

'Well, how much will it cost me?'

'The price will be twenty-three pounds and seventy-two pence. You get twenty minutes on the other side, then you have to get yourself back to the machine for the return journey.'

Running this arbitrary price over in my head, I open up my wallet and pull out everything I have—which adds up to twenty-three pounds and seventy-two pence. 'Hey, how did you—'

'So, if you'd like to step inside, just type in your desired date, time and destination into the keypad,' said the man, rather unctuously, 'and the machine will do the rest.'

Climbing inside, sitting on the tiny hard seat, I feel foolish. How can this possibly be real? I ask myself. But still, I punch in my desired details and coordinates, of which I also took the time to write down and record, and then I pull back the flimsy little brown curtain on my left-hand-side. Then I wait for a blast of G force or some kind of loud noise to erupt around me, but instead, nothing happens.

Annoyed at myself for having come all of this way for nothing, falling for a stupid joke, I pull the curtain back across so that I can get back out and go home. As I do so, however, a bright ray of sunlight hits my face, and the sound of tweeting birds drifts through the air. I'm at the edge of a large park, a park that I know well, and greenery surrounds me in all directions. A canopy of trees and bushes conceal the booth, hiding it from the joggers and dog walkers passing by on the path, and I step out of it, looking around with what must be a dazed expression.

Taking in this dramatic change of scenery, I've no choice but to conclude that the machine worked. This is the location that I typed into the machine, and so I have to presume that the date is accurate too: just under six months before that man in the local paper found his fortune. My desired time was 10 am, the time I used to take my morning stroll through this park before my health started to deteriorate, and the blue sky and the rising sun seem in line with this as well.

After five minutes or so of wandering through the park, I see a lone figure sat on a bench. A cold, tense feeling pulls me to a stop on the path, and I stare at him intently. It looks like me, but at the same time it doesn't. This man is fuller, healthier, rosier in the cheeks, and the sight of him hits home how much I've aged, or deteriorated, in just a few years. The deep lines that stretch over my face are not present on this other individual sitting on the bench up ahead, neither are the sagging jowls serving as cheeks, and worse still, the most painful part of it all, when he turns to look at me I can tell that he doesn't even recognise me.

'Do you mind?' I say, gesturing towards the empty space next to him.

'Not at all,' he replies, politely.

I make banal, pleasant small talk for a while, my nerves preventing me from cutting straight to the point of why I'm here. Perhaps unsurprisingly, considering the common ground that we have, the chatter goes on and on and we talk for quite some time, but during a brief pause I glance down at my watch and realise that it's been almost fifteen minutes since I emerged from the machine. Panic shoots through me, giving me the much-needed push I need to come out with what I really have to say.

'You know, I'm not really sure how to say

this, but I've actually come here today to tell you something.'

My younger self turns his head towards me. 'You have?'

'Yes. Look, I haven't got time to go into who I am and how I know you, but please, just listen to what I'm about to say because it's very important.'

Trying hard to be as clear and precise as possible, I tell him about the patch of land where the Roman coins are buried, then urge him to go and dig them up as soon as possible.

'But...why don't you want to go and get them for yourself?'

'I can't.'

'Why can't you?'

'Because I just can't! Look, please just do this for me, will you? It's for both our benefit.'

He went to speak again but stopped, pausing as these words sank in. And once they did, his eyes grew as wide as saucers.

'*Both* our benefit? Hey! Who are you?'

'Don't worry about who I am, just make sure you get those coins,' I plead.

After taking another look at my watch, I swiftly rise from the bench and take off across the grass, hobbling along as quickly as I can. I can hear him calling after me, yelling at me from the bench, but I ignore him and keep on going. By the time I reach the clearing I have about one minute left, and I'm in a wild panic.

The booth is right in front of me where I left it, its roof already coated in a layer of leaves and pollen from the hanging branches overhead, and I climb into it and pull the curtain back across. An excitement runs through me that I haven't felt in years, and as I sit there and count down the last remaining seconds I actually feel alive again, alive with a rush of curiosity and wonder about what I might be going back to. When I get down to the last second, I close my eyes tightly and grit my teeth.

△△△

A knocking sound wakes me from a daze. I'm lying in bed, sheets wrapped and tangled all around me, and my head feels fuzzy. With a grunt I lean over and look at the clock on my bedside table, realising that I must've over-slept. Somebody's knocking on my front door, and as consciousness slowly comes back to me I also hear their voice calling through the letter box.

'Arthur? Are you OK in there? It's Mrs Clark.'

'Err, yes!' I call out. 'Hang on, I'll just be a minute.'

My head feels worse than usual, and as I clamber around my bedroom looking for something to wear, I try to organise my disjointed thoughts. Strange images flash behind my eyes, scenes from a bizarre dream that I must've had. With a depressed sigh I realise that my illness must be worsening, my confusion and delirium now infecting my sleep. Once dressed I limp out into the hallway and make my way to the front door, grateful for the fact that Mrs Clark is here to help me get through the day.

The young woman stands by the front of the house, adjusting her hairband and name tag. The name tag reads "Mrs Clark", the alias that she and her cronies came up with when planning this job. She feels cool, calm and collective while she waits for the old man to open the door, her nervousness long gone. She knows the routine well now as she's done it many times before, her act refined and perfected. Being part of a criminal cartel, she has no problem at all getting her hands on restricted pharmaceutical products, nor has she any reservations about illegally administering them. Where money is involved, "Mrs Clark's" kind will go to all kinds of extreme lengths to get to it.

When it was announced in the paper a few years ago that a local man had acquired a fortune it soon piqued the interest of her gang, but with the money safely stashed away in the man's ultra-secure bank account it seemed like there was no way to get to it. With cyber crime and online fraud being rife the advanced security procedures in place were often too tricky to get around, even for well-organised, professional criminals like them. For this job they had to get creative and come up with a new method, a unique approach that required a large degree of patience and commitment.

Convincing the man that he was sick wasn't actually too difficult. They'd got their hands on a secondhand private ambulance and some uniforms, then spent a few weeks quietly watching him, learning his daily routine. Once they were familiar with his habits and actions they followed him during one of his walks, staying discreetly out of sight in their ambulance until he passed under a dark flyover with no cameras. Then, once he was in position, they pulled up next to him, jumped out, and chloroformed him. They kept him captive for a couple of days before taking him home, pumping him full of amnesia-inducing drugs. By the time they eventually took him back to his house, wheeling him up the driveway on a wheelchair, his mind was a mess and he was putty in their hands. Mrs Clark soon became part of his new routine, a permanent feature of his new life, and he never questioned her credentials.

Siphoning the cash from his bank account was a much more tedious, boring task. The security measures weren't that hard to get around as long as Arthur was a willing participant in his "mental exercises". Fingerprint ID?—no problem. Voice recognition?—piece of cake. Retinal scan—easy. The only security measure they couldn't get around was the maximum daily transfer limit, hence the need for Mrs Clark's endless visits. But this was OK; extreme amounts of cash called for extreme measures, and this was simply one of them.

There's another knock on the door as I search around for my keys. It's locked from the inside, and I need my keys to open it. At last I find them, stashed away in my coat pocket in the cupboard, and I put one in the lock and turn it. Mrs Clark is standing there as I open the door, her pleasant face beaming me its usual sympathetic smile. With my brain lost in its usual dizziness, I urge her to come in. How grateful I am for her company and care.

THE SOUL
DESTROYER

He ventured into the tropics, to study a parasite
And while he was out in the jungle, he had an awful fright
Whatever it was that he saw, it certainly took its toll
It sucked away his will to live, and then it destroyed his soul

T he car pulled up at the curb in the middle of the sleepy, residential street, then came to a gentle stop. On each side of the road, amid the neat rows of trees trailing off into the distance in either direction, brown semi-detached houses sat behind their well-tended gardens and tidy driveways. When the driver's door opened a stout, suited man climbed out, his neatly-combed head turning left and right as he looked for a door number. Once he found what he was looking for, he straightened his tie and proceeded to walk up one of the gravel driveways, his polished shoes crunching the small stones as he went.

Inspector Griffin was the Chief Inspector at HCQ, the organisation responsible for investigating hospitals and mental institutions across the UK. His visit to this leafy, suburban street was regarding an ongoing investigation at Bryson Psychiatric Hospital, a secure facility for the mentally ill situated out in the Kentish countryside. It'd been a very bad few months for the hospital, what with an unusually large amount of staff members either leaving or being struck off sick. A wave of resignations and sicknesses of this size and magnitude was virtually unheard of, and so it soon prompted an investigation.

The address he'd just arrived at belonged to a nurse who was currently on sick leave from Bryson Hospital due to severe stress and anxiety, and according to the latest reports her condition wasn't getting any better. Her situation was beginning to become a very common one for nurses working at this particular facility. Just a few days ago, Griffin had visited the home of another nurse who'd swallowed a bottle of painkillers in an attempt to end her own life. She'd been in a catatonic state when he'd arrived, her family attending to her needs and feeding her, and so his efforts to get some useful information from her had been futile. He'd sat there in that house for over an hour, listening to the woman's distraught husband describe her strange behaviour while she herself sat in the corner staring out of the window, her glazed, unblinking eyes filled with a haunted look that Griffin could still see now in his mind's eye. He'd listened as her relatives described in detail the wails and cries that came out of her room at night, as well as informing him that they now had to keep all sharp objects and harmful medicines hidden from her at all times. After making some notes and thanking the family for their time, he'd left the house with a deep-set belief that the nurse was never going to return to work again.

Despite the peculiar nature of this recent spate of absences and resignations, its actual cause wasn't a complete mystery. Griffin knew the basic reason why the staff members were leaving and falling ill, but at the same time he just couldn't quite believe it. Several senior nurses and lower-level managers were being very bold and forthright about their opinions and theories, but neither Griffin nor his seniors at HCQ could take them seriously. Most of them were claiming that employees were leaving due to a new patient who'd been admitted to the hospital five months ago, and that a brief look into his eyes was all it took for one to lose their mind.

Griffin found all of this ridiculous, but at the same time he had to acknowledge that this new patient was indeed a unique case. The man was a biologist, specialising in parasitology, with a distinguished career; he was Cambridge educated, had several scientific articles in well-respected journals published under his name, a list of degrees and accolades as long as his arm, and a legacy within the scientific community that even Charles Darwin or Isaac Newton would have been proud of. Griffin doubted that any mental institution in the land had ever had anyone of such status under their roof, and his sectioning was indeed an enigma.

The biologist, known to all as Professor Avery, was sectioned under the mental health act following a state-funded work expedition in the tropics of South America. Griffin had personally gone through his hospital file with a fine-tooth comb, reading everything he could about him. Details of the work expedition were fortunately available for him to read, and he'd scoured them obsessively, trying to gain some kind of clue as to what had happened. According to the files, Professor Avery had travelled to a jungle region of Panama to study a certain type of parasitic nematode. A small team of coworkers and biology students had flown out there with him to assist him in the process of recording data, but Avery had been the main figurehead of the project.

It became apparent after reading the file that the professor had seen something out there that had caused him to lose his mind, making him lose his grip on reality. Officers from a tiny local constabulary out in a Central American village were called when locals reported a foreign man behaving erratically and attacking several residents, and additional charges were put forward after the professor made violent advances towards officers in the station. Photographs of bite marks on one officer's arm were attached to the report for Griffin to see, as was the bruising to one officer's face who had to open Avery's cell door when he attempted to hang himself with his own belt. UK officials had been called in to assist with Avery's deportation, and several more violent outbursts had been recorded during the process.

Since his arrival at Bryson Hospital, however, Avery had slipped into a prolonged bout of silence and withdrawal, with not one single word being heard from him during the five months of his incarceration. He refused to eat, drink or communicate with anyone, but despite the adoption of this antisocial behaviour there had been no reports of abusive or threatening behaviour of any kind, no cases of injuries sustained to any of the nurses who tended to him. On paper the professor was a harmless patient, a physical threat to no one, but his presence within the hospital was still dangerous somehow. Trauma and torment seemed to ooze from his every pore, and those who had gazed into his deep-set, wizened eyes claimed to have felt his pain on a kind of telepathic level. And as if this wasn't strange enough, these claims went even further still. One nurse in particular, the second one to resign after the professor's arrival, claimed to have seen a mental image after making eye contact with him, as though some kind of grainy picture had been transferred across to her through his stare.

Indeed, it was this atmosphere that Avery had created within the facility that was supposedly responsible for the numerous resignations and absences, this profound effect that he had on those in his close vicinity. Griffin had not yet been granted permission to see Professor

Avery in person due to this risk of health, but apparently, according to certain rumours, his face was now permanently covered up to prevent any more incidents of this nature. Descriptions of some kind of bag had been spoken of unofficially, a kind of thin veil secured around his head and neck to protect nurses from his dangerous stare. In addition to this the professor was on constant suicide watch, the small metal hatch on his cell door left open to allow the wardens a clear view of his movements and actions.

Putting aside the brief, violent outbursts in Central America surrounding his arrest, Professor Avery didn't seem to want to do anyone any harm; his suicidal tendencies were simply contagious to those around him whether he wanted them to be or not, and it was for this reason that he was considered to be a very dangerous man.

Griffin approached the front door of the suburban house, then rang the bell. After a few moments a blurred figure appeared behind the stained glass, then a polite, unassuming man opened the door and welcomed him in.

'She's upstairs,' said the man, who was obviously the nurse's husband. 'Do you want to go up and see her?'

'Yes please,' said Griffin, before following him up a dim, carpeted staircase.

'I'm not sure how much you'll be able to get out of her. She's been very quiet today.'

'What has she told you?' whispered Griffin, lowering his voice as the two of them reached the upper landing.

'Very little. She's hardly spoken to me at all since it all happened. In fact, she speaks more in her sleep than she does during her waking hours.' The man paused for a second, rubbing the bags under his eyes. 'There are noises in the early hours of the morning: screams, yells, swearing. She sleeps in the spare room now. It's...It's better that way.'

'She has nightmares?'

'Every night.'

'Do you know what they're about?'

'Every time I try to speak to her, she switches off.'

Griffin noticed a faint quiver in his voice, a light trembling, and decided not to press him any further. The distress of it all was evident on his face, the screams and sleepless nights had etched lines around his brow and temple.

'Where's the...spare room?'

'It's over there,' he said, nodding his head towards the end of the hallway.

'Thank you.'

The woman's husband forced a smile, then skulked back towards the staircase. As soon as he was out of sight Griffin put his ear to the bedroom door and listened closely for any sounds.

Hearing none, he then knocked on it a couple of times. The room sounded echoey from the other side, his knocks ringing through the air for longer than they should have. Out of politeness and courtesy he waited a long time for a reply, but, hearing none, he eventually turned the handle and let himself in.

The room was bare and empty, with just a single bed and a chair in the corner. The curtains were half-drawn, casting a faint grey light over everything, and the air was still. A woman was lying on the bed, her head propped up with two pillows and her body covered with a thin bedsheet. She didn't move or stir when Griffin entered the room, nor was there any noticeable change in her blank expression. He almost felt alone as he walked in and stood by the end of the bed, like he was in a room with a mannequin or a waxwork model in a museum. Eventually, after several polite attempts to communicate with her, he quietly sat himself down on the chair in the corner, watching her the whole time.

Her face was so pale that it blended and merged with the pillow, her pinky-red bloodshot eyes the only thing with any real colour to them. She was floating somewhere between consciousness and unconsciousness, awake and not awake, lost in her own lonely realm. In fact, she was so utterly unresponsive and unmoved to Griffin's presence that he wondered, for a brief second, whether she might have passed away without her husband knowing. This suspicion didn't last too long, however, because upon close inspection he could see that a slight tremor ran through her body at regular intervals, a kind of shudder that shook her torso and made the bedframe creak. It was so minute and subtle that it could've easily been missed, but now that he was close to her he could see it.

'What happened to you? What made you ill?' he whispered into her ear.

There was no response to these words, no flicker or flinch in her countenance.

'Did Professor Avery do this to you?'

The faint creaking of the bed frame was still the only sound in the room, but even so, Griffin detected some kind of shift after he'd mentioned the professor's name, some alteration deep within her.

'Did you...interact with him in any way?'

Now there was noticeable movement; so noticeable, in fact, that it made Griffin jump. The nurse's breathing became heavier and audible, her chest rising and falling under the sweaty sheets. He was sure that she could hear him now, sure that he wasn't just talking to himself. It was the mention of the professor's name that had initially gotten through to her, so he deliberately mentioned it again in an effort to open her up some more.

'Did you...look at Professor Avery?'

A pinprick of light glistened from somewhere in the pale folds of her face, and Griffin realised, with tense surprise, that it was a tear in the corner of her eye. The grey light seeping in through the curtains was just bright enough to reflect against it, exposing some inner emotion the nurse was evidently experiencing. She was about to crack, and Griffin moved in closer.

'Speak to me. Nobody can help you unless you speak to them.'

Her thin lips began to tremble and blubber, and with a weak cry she said, 'There...There's no helping this.'

'There's no helping what?'

Her face was screwed up in pain now, and she turned her head towards the window.

'What did he do to you?'

'He didn't...He didn't do anything,' she sobbed. 'He just...made me see.'

'See what?'

The tears were rolling down her cheeks now, and she brought one of her hands up from under the covers to wipe them. As she did so, a pungent odour wafted out across the room, hitting home the fact that she hadn't washed or left the bed in days. Her torment was detectable in every aspect of her being; when she spoke, it was like she was speaking from the depths of a deep cave within her mind, a cave that she'd carved out for herself to escape whatever was haunting her.

'I...I won't talk about it! I won't! It's...It's just too horrible!'

'How did he make you see? How did he do it?'

The tears and chokes were coming on strong now, too strong for the woman to answer coherently, but Griffin wasn't going to give up.

'Did you look into his eyes?'

In between the heaving sobs and shudders, the nurse managed to nod her head in confirmation.

'And then what? What happened when you looked into his eyes?'

'They...They were just so full of...misery. The...The way he looked at me...sucking me into those two black pits!'

'And what did you see? Tell me what you saw!'

The nurse was now hysterical. Her sobs had turned into high-pitched wails and cries, echoing around the bare, empty room and shaking the walls. The door burst open unexpectedly, and the woman's husband leaned in with a stern look about him.

'I think that's enough,' he said. 'She's not well enough for this.'

With the nurse shaking and hollering next to him as she was, Griffin couldn't protest. He rose from the small chair and made his way out, leaving the husband to tend to her.

Outside, standing by his car next to the road, he could still hear the woman's screams.

Visiting the two nurses had had an unsettling effect on Griffin. He'd still been very sceptical after seeing the first one, despite her chronic state, but after seeing both of them and witnessing their compounded trauma and distress firsthand, he was left with no choice but to at least consider the far-fetched theory that the professor was somehow contaminating people with his thoughts. Whether there was a supernatural element to any of it, he couldn't be sure, but there was certainly no denying the fact that the two employees had seen something whilst in his presence—something that'd destroyed their souls and made them lose the will to live.

He knew what had to be done next. It was an inevitable, unavoidable task that simply had to be endured if he was to get to the bottom of this case and put it to bed: he was going to have to visit the hospital and meet Professor Avery in person. The senior staff at Bryson Hospital had not been allowing any visits to the professor for quite some time now, not even to HCQ inspectors, but with enough persistence on Griffin's part, combined with a firm letter from the Chief Executive, he knew that they would have to eventually give in. Sitting in his home study, in front of his thick wooden desk piled high with folders, Griffin resolved to get this process in motion today. First though, before he could even begin to prepare himself for the daunting, intimidating prospect of meeting Professor Avery in the flesh, he wanted to go through his file one more time.

He had a decent amount of information at his disposal, a large stack of papers about an inch thick. The sequence of events that'd happened during the professor's expedition were already known to him, almost committed to memory in fact, but Griffin wanted to learn a bit more about the actual parasite that Avery was studying at the time. Flicking through the assortment of papers, he found the typed up notes that the professor had made prior to, and during, his expedition.

He read slowly and carefully, taking his time, eager to learn more about this bizarre creature.

Classification: Parasitic nematode/roundworm.

Habitat: Tropical forests of Central America/South America.

Known hosts: Cephalotes Atratus Ant. Bananaquit bird. Tryant flycatcher bird.

Life cycle: The host ant, Cephalotes Atratus, gets infected by the nematode after eating the infected fecal matter of either the Bananaquit bird or the

Tryant flycatcher bird. Once infected the ant falls prey to the parasite, displaying a sluggishness and change in behaviour. As well as this, the ant will also take on a physical change in appearance. It's abdomen (usually black in colour) will swell up in size (due to being filled with nematode eggs) and take on a bright shade of red, then, after this transformation of its body is complete, the ant will feel compelled to climb up a long blade of grass in the near vicinity and stick its red swollen abdomen up in the air. To passing birds (namely the Bananaquit and Tyrant) the ant's swollen abdomen will strongly resemble a ripe berry, tempting the bird to swoop down and consume it. Once the bird has been tricked into eating this infected section of the ant's body, the eggs will pass through its body and get excreted out, therefore spreading the eggs out into further ant colonies.

Griffin slapped the papers back down on his desk, then ran a hand through his hair. He was at a loss at what to make of this. This parasite, or nematode, or whatever it was, sounded vile, but he still couldn't imagine how or why someone would go insane after seeing it. The professor had completely lost it out there in the Central American tropics, running around attacking people like a wild man, and although the details of this ant-infecting parasite were ghastly and horrid, they just couldn't account for such dramatic behaviour.

Pulling out his phone, he scrolled down until he found the Chief Executive's number. He knew that he would have to get the professor to open up to him if he was to solve this riddle, but before that could happen the Chief Executive would have to persuade Bryson Hospital to allow a visit.

△△△

The psychiatric facility had a cold, austere look to it, the iron gates and brown brickwork completely unwelcoming and featureless. There was a still, silent feel to the air, and as Griffin parked his car he looked up at the rows of reinforced glass windows, wondering whether the atmosphere was any better inside. The receptionist told him to sit down and wait for a senior nurse who'd escort him through the building, and he did so without complaint.

The senior nurse was a petite woman with mousy hair and a familiar-sounding voice. Griffin had never met her before, but was sure that he'd spoken to her over the phone at some point. She was accompanied by a heavyset man who wore a similar white uniform to hers, and after a brief exchange the three of them swiped through a set of security doors and made their way down towards the maximum security wing.

'The professor's been transferred to maximum security following the recent problems,' said the nurse, as they walked down a sterile-looking white corridor with cells on either side. 'He's not displayed any violent behaviour, but...well, he's proven himself to be a threat in his own way.'

'So I've heard,' replied Griffin.

'We've also taken the precaution of covering up his face. This may seem a little unnecessary, but we think it's a sensible move.'

'So it's true then?'

'I'm sorry?'

'It's true that you're covering up his face?'

'Inspector Griffin, we had to do something. Several staff members have fallen ill after looking—'

'I know, I know,' said Griffin, interjecting her in a polite way so she didn't have to go through all

of the grizzly details, 'I just wasn't sure whether it was true or not. There's no mention of it in the report.

'It's a spit hood,' she said, candidly. 'It's a thin mesh spit hood. It doesn't cause him any discomfort of any kind, other than maybe restricting his vision a little bit.'

'Has he been cooperative with this decision?'

'Yes, he certainly has. He hasn't protested about anything since he's been here.'

Griffin nodded, thoughtfully. 'And he's still not speaking to anyone?'

'No. You don't get a single word out of him all day. He's been here for five months now, and I don't even know what he sounds like.'

'So, have people tried speaking to him?'

'We did when he first arrived, but...' The woman's voice trailed off for a second. '...but not any more.'

They walked the rest of the way in silence, an uneasiness lingering between them as they descended further down into the building.

It took about five minutes to reach the professor's cell. Griffin knew that he'd arrived before being told, the open hatch on the metal door being the main giveaway. There were two other beefy- looking male nurses outside the cell, one crouching down to look through the hatch. The men had obviously been informed of Griffin's visit, because they prepared themselves to open the door without being told, one fumbling for a key on his hip, the other searching for a set of restraints in his pocket. Once everything was in place and the key was being inserted into the lock, the senior nurse turned towards Griffin with a serious look in her eye.

'Don't get too close to him. As I said, he's not known to be violent, but you've seen the damage he can do to people.'

'Yes,' said Griffin, trying his best to cover up his shaking hands.

Sensing his nervousness, she then added, 'We'll be right here the whole time,' before dutifully giving a nod to the big nurse with the key.

The lock snapped open, the door opened wide, and Griffin, sweating under his shirt collar, took a few deep breaths and then entered.

The cell was at a contrast to the corridor outside. It was dim and stale, with just a single overhead bulb for light. A dark mound sat slumped in the corner, shrouded in shadow, and Griffin stood there for a few long moments watching it, paralysed with tension and fear. The professor looked thin and frail under the hospital slacks, his delicate frame barely visible under the baggy folds. His head was no different, of course, the mesh hood concealing everything from the neck up. It was unclear whether the professor actually knew he was there or not, as there'd been no movement from him at all. The mesh spit hood sat over his head like a starched pillowcase, giving absolutely nothing away, its stiff creases concealing its contents.

The silence in the cell was so all-encompassing, so total and complete, that it felt wrong for Griffin to break it, but he had to start somewhere.

'Professor Avery?' he said, squinting into the shadows.

The words came out as a croaky whisper, and he had to clear his throat before he went on. 'I'm Inspector Griffin, Chief Inspector at HCQ. May I speak to you?'

He received nothing by way of reply. Complete silence resumed, broken only by the faint sound of distant shouting from somewhere down the corridor outside.

'Do you mind if I sit down?'

There was no response, but at the same time there was no objection either, so he sat down and leaned back against the opposite wall. There was still a safe distance of about seven feet between them, but Griffin was now close enough to see the professor more clearly, the shapes and contours of his form coming into focus. The thin veil of the hood did its job of hiding the professor's face, but rather worryingly, it didn't obscure it completely. Bony, chiselled features were discernible through its thin material, and Griffin had to make a constant conscientious effort not to stare at them for too long. The dim outlines and crevices enshrouded within the hood were so starved and gaunt in their appearance that they vaguely resembled a skull rather than a living human head, the bridge of the nose and cheek bones protruding through pale skin.

'Will you talk to me, Professor?'

Again, there was not as much as a flicker of response.

'What happened to you, Professor? What did you see out in the tropics?'

It was hard to believe that this introverted, crumpled figure opposite him was the same man that Griffin had read about. The numerous mentions of exemplary conduct rose up to the forefront of his mind, graduation photographs accompanied by pages of accolades, acclaimed published scientific articles, too many degree certificates to count, and it all came from this mute, incarcerated mess sitting before him, this absolute wreck of a human being. His fear was rapidly turning into sympathy the longer he sat there opposite Avery, but at the same time, the memory of the two sick nurses he'd seen forced him to keep his guard up.

'I want to understand what happened to you. I'm not here to judge you on anything. Why don't you talk to me?'

Another bout of silence tested Griffin's patience even further, but he wasn't done yet.

'I've read a lot about your career, Professor. There are many people out there who have much praise for you.'

For a split second Griffin thought he saw movement in the professor's hands, a slight tremble running all the way down to the fingernails that'd been chewed to stumps. It could've just been a trick of the light, however, because nothing else followed it. Five minutes passed by, then ten, with Griffin trying his hardest to break through the thick wall that the professor had built around himself, but it was to no avail. Reaching his limit of patience and perseverance, he made a few loose notes for the disappointing report he would have to produce at some point later in the day, then slowly got up and rose to his feet. Turning to the professor one last time, he looking down at him with genuine sorrow and pity.

'Nobody can help you unless you talk to them, Avery. Just think about that.'

With a deep, heart-felt sigh, he finally walked away from the cloaked figure on the ground, making his way back over towards the cell door. With all hopes of solving the mystery dwindled away to nothing, he raised his hand up to give the steel door a couple of knocks. The knocks never came, however, because just as he was raising his hand, curling it up into a fist, the most pained voice he'd ever heard in his life rose up from somewhere behind him.

'He...He was still alive when I found him.'

It was so unexpected that for a few seconds he thought he must've been hearing things. Slowly and methodically, he turned back around, staring wide-eyed at the lonesome figure on the floor.

'What?' he whispered. 'What did you say?'

There was definitely movement down there now, a thin trembling inside the hospital gowns, just strong enough to make out through the murky dinge.

'He...He was...He was still alive.'

The voice went straight through Griffin, straight through to his core. Everything about its pitch and tone was laced with hurt, loaded and oozing with pain. Retracing his steps, he walked back along the middle of the cell, back to where he was previously sitting.

'Who was still alive? Who are you talking about?' he asked, planting himself back down on the dusty ground.

Two dark sockets stared out at him from the depths of the hood, two smudges as black as coal, but something had shifted in them now, some spark of life had been ignited.

'You...You want to know what happened?'

'Yes! Yes, I do! Tell me, Professor.'

'No. No, you don't. Y...You—'

'I want to know what happened Professor, and I want to help you. So tell me.'

A considerable amount of time passed before the professor spoke again. Shakes and tremors were still visible under the gowns, and the faint outline of his delicate jaw jutted up and down as though he was searching for some lost reservoir of strength that might've existed within him. He must've found some somewhere, because the words eventually came;

they were strained and agonising to listen to, but they came.

'I...I was in a village one day during my expedition, out in Central America. It was a tiny little place, no more than a few dozen huts...'

It felt so strange for Griffin to sit there and hear Professor Avery speak. His voice sounded just as withered and hollow as his body looked; inhuman, almost. He remained as silent as a mouse as he listened to it, however, not wanting to disrupt the flow.

'The heat...it was so intense that day, and we'd been out in it for hours. We had a guide, my...my team and I. He was an indigenous man local to the area, and he...he'd arranged a place for us to stay. We were all sweating and...and dehydrated, so none of us protested when we got to the village in the afternoon with a view to settling down early for the day. We all had notes to write up anyway, so we saw it as an opportunity to catch up with some work and recuperate.'

There was a lengthy pause from the professor. His pale, gaunt visage was hung down towards the cell floor in deep contemplation. Griffin was still completely silent, making only rough notes here and there.

'It was a beautiful place, in its...in its own way. These huts sat along the edge of a warm river, wild palm trees and long grass as far as the eye could see. The natives were so hos...hospitable....so...so welcoming.'

The mention of the native's hospitality caused the professor's voice to dip and falter even more, and Griffin sensed a touch of shame in there as well.

'Th...They cooked food for us, prepared a big meal. It...It should've been a delightful evening, but...but there was something bothering the villagers, some kind of bad atmosphere in the air. We all noticed it, and I...I eventually ended up asking the guide what was wrong. We were starting to get paranoid. We...We began to wonder whether it was something we'd done.'

It was hard for Griffin to tell whether the professor was actually looking at him or not, or whether he'd even looked at him at all since he'd entered the room. The hood sat over his head like a baggy fly net, continually reducing his features down to a vague blur.

Realising that he'd fallen silent again, Griffin gently coaxed him on. 'And what was it? What was wrong?'

'It turned out that...that the problem wasn't anything to do with us, exactly. A child h...had gone missing from the village, and they were worrying over him. He'd disappeared the evening before, and...'

'And what?' whispered Griffin, as the professor drifted off into yet another bout of silence.

'...and...nobody had seen him since.'

'And then what? What happened next?'

'After dinner we...we all retired for the night. It was still early, probably about seven o' clock, and it was still light, but we all went back to our little shacks that they'd...that they'd kindly prepared for us. It felt so good to lie down. I...I didn't have much of a bed in there, but to me, at...at that moment, it was like a luxury hotel. My legs were aching from days of trekking through the jungle, j...just resting there on the thin bed was bliss. I eventually began sorting out some notes I'd made over the previous few days. I was just lying there, putting everything in order.'

'Notes about the parasite, you mean?'

'Yes. That...That thing.'

The professor's twig-like fingers clutched at his knees at the mention of the parasite, as though he was speaking about something that went beyond evil.

'And then what?'

'I was busy organising my notes, and then...then this...this noise drifted in from outside. At first I thought it was an animal, a...a bird, maybe. It was like a.. a high-pitched wailing coming from somewhere out in the trees, a whining sound in the distance that drifted in through the open window of my hut. I seemed to be the only one who could hear it. I...I eventually got up and had a look outside, and...and there was nothing there, nobody else around. B...But still, this horrible noise went on and on, and I...I just had to find out what it was. It seemed to be coming from...from the river, so I headed in that direction, following my ear. The evening was just beginning to close in by this point, and the sky was shifting into a deep, deep amber. I still had plenty of light, but...but I also knew that I had to move briskly, nonetheless. After pushing through the long grass for a while I could see the river appearing up ahead of me, the gentle waves reflecting through the foliage. The...The screaming had also grown more acute, and...and I could tell by this point that it was coming from somewhere up in the trees. F...Following this sickly noise, I...I ended up at the base of a dead tree by the river embankment, a flaking old thing with not a single leaf on it. The faint squeals were...were coming from somewhere up in this tree, and now that I was close, I could...I could tell that they were...'

'They were what?'

'They were...human.'

Griffin's handwriting was becoming messy as he continued to jot down his notes, his fingers shaky and out of his control. 'What happened next?' he said, after scrawling down the last word.

'T...There was a shape in the tree up above me. A...A round silhouette set against the amber sky. I stared at it for some time, knowing deep down what it was but...but not wanting to believe it. It was a child! No more than...than six or seven years old! He was up there in this tree...c...clinging on to one of the dead branches about thirty feet up, wailing and...wailing. His pudgy little arms and legs were wrapped around this branch and it was...it was dangling over the river! I...I have no idea how he managed to get up there, but...but there he was, as naked as the day he was born, screaming and yelling up into the dimming sky. I thought about calling for help, but...but I couldn't risk startling him and making him fall. Instead I...I silently began climbing up the tree myself, grabbing on to the flakes of dry bark and hauling myself up. It took me five minutes or so to get up there, but...but I did, and...'

'And what did you see?' Griffin whispered, watching the blurred, shadowy recesses of the professor's countenance as he relived his story.

'And...it was the strangest thing. T...There was no movement coming from him at all. The screams continued to come, th...they came in abundance, but...but his body was stiff and rigid. He was as still as a statue up there! Like a screaming statue! And...And there were flies on him! Dozens and dozens of flies! They were buzzing and crawling all over his little body! Buzzing all over him as he...as he clung onto this flaking branch!'

The professor was moving now, moving more than he had done so since Griffin had entered the cell. His thin arms were wrapped around his knees, hugging them tightly, and he began to rock backwards and forwards in erratic jolts, like a trauma victim pulled away from the scene of a fresh accident. His gasps and sobs shook the stiff folds of the spit hood, giving it the appearance of a deflated balloon caught in the wind.

'I...I had to get closer to him. I had to do something! Up until this point I...I'd only seen him from behind. I was looking up at him from some lower branches, look...looking up towards the back of his neck and head. The...The branches were getting thinner the further up I climbed, but...but I had to get up there. I...I almost fell into the river at one point, standing on a dry branch that snapped as soon as I put my foot on it, but...but I carried on. Wh...When I finally got up to his level I was...I was clinging on for dear life! The river glistened and splashed underneath me. It was...It was so far down.'

'What had happened to the boy, Professor?'

The hood bobbed and shook in time with the professor's tremors; he was hugging himself tighter and tighter, rocking further and further. With a strained voice, he continued.

'It was like...it was like an invisible force was holding him in place up there, gluing his body in this rigid fashion. He...He was screaming but he wasn't moving. Not even his face. And...And it was then that I saw them! H...His eyes! Oh, god, his eyes! They were open wide, looking up towards the distant clouds over-head, but...but they were...'

'They were what?'

'They...They were hideous! Big, red and bulbous! His face and eyes were...it was a scene from a nightmare! W...Worse than anything anyone could imagine! I...I was close at this point, high up in the tree, and...and I could see it all. S...Something was going on under the surface of his eyes. S...Something was writhing and...and wriggling!'

'Wriggling?'

'Eggs! Eggs and larvae! They were crawling around in his eyes! H...Hundreds of them! Th...They were moving around in there! Swimming and...and moving around!'

Griffin suddenly felt nauseous. A sickness rose up in his gut, a sickness so intense that he had to put down his notepad and pen so that he could lay a hand over his stomach.

'You're not honestly saying that the parasite...'

'The parasite was in him! It'd infected him! I...I still have no idea how it could've happened. M...Maybe he drank some infected water somewhere, or...or ate some bird droppings from the ground, I don't know, but...but the point is is that somehow that *thing* managed to get inside him so that it could use him as a vehicle. It swelled his eyes and made them bulbous, turning his once-white sclera bright red. As red as...as red as...cherries.'

Griffin was silent. He felt giddy, and the room seemed to tilt and turn around him.

'But...But the worst part of it all was...was that there was still life in those young eyes! There was still a person looking out of them! And...And as I hung there, holding onto the thin branches of that dead tree, he suddenly...he suddenly turned those red eyes towards me! He was looking at me! Oh, god, he was looking at me with those eyes! He...He could see me there next to him, but...but he couldn't move from his branch. His stubby arms and legs were glued in place, stiff as boards...he was...he was trapped inside his little body. That moment when...that moment when I caught his gaze... when our eyes met, it was just... His pupils were like...were like tiny black islands in seas of red larvae...moving, bubbling, writhing red seas. He was...he was fully conscious in there, looking out at me through this hive of eggs! I kept telling myself that it couldn't be true, couldn't be real, but...but there it was! Right in front of me! And...And then...'

Avery slipped into another bout of silence, another pause, but Griffin couldn't bring himself to urge him on any further, as his own voice was now reduced to a mere croak. He could do little more than wait and watch the professor, unconsciously bringing his own knees up to his chest as if mirroring his pose.

'...then there was a flash of movement, a...a flurry of wings and feathers.'

'Oh, no,' mumbled Griffin, only to himself.

'When...When that bird came down and plucked at him he was looking right at me! That eye was looking at me as it was pecked open, the beak sinking straight into the soft jelly, sending eggs dribbling down his cheek. It...It was...'

There was some kind of eruption within the professor's hood, some kind of gurgling explosion. Suddenly, in less than a second, the thin mesh was sprayed from the inside with a rush of vomit, the hot liquid collecting into a pool as the professor hung his head over his knees. Two scrawny hands reached up and took hold of the dripping fabric, clutching it like talons. With a quick sharp tug, a reflex action, the professor ripped the wet hood from over his bony head, bile dangling from its folds. His sunken features were now completely visible and exposed, the yellow light of the overhead bulb illuminating his scalp and chiselled temples.

By the time Griffin realised he was looking into the professor's uncovered eyes, it was too late. When the hood came off he'd been unable to look away, unable to divert his gaze. Like a motorist driving past the scene of a nasty accident and turning his head to take a look, he'd feasted his eyes on the spectacle before him, gorging greedily on its horrors. With the veil gone the professor's face emanated something that could be felt but not described, an icy coldness that put an invisible hook in you. Up until this point the horrid description of what the professor had seen in the tropics had been confined to the medium of words, limiting the extent to which Griffin could visualise it and understand it, but now, with that face, that expression, right there in front of him in the cell, he could somehow *see* what the professor had been describing, as though the very image itself was carved into the contours of his skin.

He felt himself slipping, falling, descending down into a hole. He was sinking down under an incredible weight, the weight of the image that'd just been transferred to him, the image that no human should be forced to endure, and he had to fight against it to keep himself above ground. Fists thrashing and lashing at the air, he struck out at this evil presence consuming him, fighting back against the horrific vision that was pushing him down. At first his hands and feet made no contact with anything, his punches and kicks stabbing at empty space, but then his blows began to land on targets, his knuckles striking the tall forms that'd gathered around him in a circle. Lashing out with frenzied fervour, he pounded away at these big white apparitions, attacking with all his might. With this vivid picture glowing and shining in front of him, haunting him with its detail, he was fighting for his life to get away from it, fighting for his very sanity, putting all of his strength into every punch and blow.

But then a tiny stabbing sensation put an end to his struggle, a single pin-prick to his neck that penetrated the softness of his skin. He wasn't sinking anymore, now he was being lifted up, lifted up higher and higher by these mysterious towering white forms, their strong arms carrying his limp body away from the dust and grime of the cell floor.

△△△

The room was dim, silent and grey. Griffin didn't know where he was, but he couldn't afford to try and work it out either. There was a dull ache stretching across his body, throbbing away in his back, but this too could be granted no attention. Neither could the fact that his old clothes were gone, replaced with a thin baggy gown that covered his trembling body like a crumpled tent. There was only one thing that he could concentrate on now, one solitary thing that he could afford to exert his energy into: pushing the image out of his mind. It wanted dearly to enter his psyche, to penetrate the walls of his cranium, and its determination was relentless. Every ounce of his strength, every fibre of his being, went into the task of keeping this horrific picture away, and diverting his attention away from it for as long as possible.

He'd been like this for hours now, pushing it away, forcing it back, trying his best to look away from it. He was like a cornered mouse in his own mind, trapped, trying desperately to fend off the menacing claws of a hungry cat. He felt as though he was fighting a losing battle, but his survival instinct wouldn't let him give up. *But how long can I actually keep this up for?* he wondered, as he sat on the floor of this strange new room, his head aching from the constant strain. And he had *seen* it after all, hadn't he? He'd seen the image projected from the professor's eyes, seen its potent content, so wasn't it already lodged deep in his brain? Wasn't it already too firmly embedded in his synapses to erase? Surely it was, surely he was now stuck with it for the rest of his days, stuck with it shouting for his attention night and day with its sadistical intent?

Yes, Griffin concluded. How could he possibly keep this up? The image, the picture, wanted him too much, its desire and hunger was simply too great. With a torturous cry, reaching his personal limit, Griffin finally cracked and buckled under the immense mental pressure bearing down upon him, letting the sickly, haunting image invade his senses and consume him, swallowing him whole. And just like that, as he gave in to it, as he gave up the fight, all of the tension and struggling vanished. Leaning back against the hard concrete wall, the wall of this room he found himself in, his body slumped and his face sagged at the edges. Now that he'd succumbed to the image, letting himself get eaten and swallowed by it, all of his energy and life force drained away into nothingness. His past life, everything that he had ever wanted, everything that he formerly yearned for or lusted after, suddenly seemed pointless and trivial, nothing more than childish dreams. The image now hung like a curtain across his vision, a permanent backdrop against all that he saw, reducing everything else to monotony. The echoey sounds from out in the corridor sank away into tiny whispers, the stale smell of the room lost its edge, and the pain running down his back grew less acute. And then, once everything outside of the image was reduced to a mere sliver in his peripheral vision, a mere speck in his awareness, his eyes glazed over and his head craned down towards the floor in defeat.

VIRTUAL VENGEANCE

The name was Virtual Vengeance, and it went down a treat

They came from miles around, to punish the fresh meat

The ugly truth was hidden, at least not spoken of

But people loved it nonetheless, and got their rocks off!

Harvey sprinted through the dark wet city streets, looking over his shoulder every few seconds to see if the man was still chasing him. It seemed as though he'd lost him for the moment, but he knew that he had to keep on moving fast if he wanted to stay safe. He was lost and in a state of delirium, dizzy and confused, disoriented like he'd never been before. The streets and lanes looked familiar but alien, recognisable but unrecognisable at the same time. He didn't even know what time it was, but it was obviously pretty late because the street lamps were shining their sickly orange light over the curbs and drains, and the roads were empty apart from the occasional taxi cruising past.

This feeling of confusion and displacement was nothing new to Harvey, he'd experienced it countless times before after one of his drink and drug binges, but this time it felt more severe than usual. He had no idea how he got here, no clear memory of anything in particular, except, of course, of the maniac who tried to attack him a few minutes earlier. The man had come out of nowhere, violently attacking him with a large baseball bat. Somehow Harvey had managed to duck and avoid the blow, sprinting away to safety as the tall man gathered and repositioned himself. It was all completely unprovoked as well, or at least it seemed to be. Harvey certainly wasn't short of enemies; in fact, he had so many now he'd literally lost count. Borrowing money and not paying it back, selling people baking soda for cocaine, stealing food and crates of beer from shops—he was guilty of it all. A petty criminal tends to accumulate a long list of enemies as the years go by, and Harvey definitely was no exception, so he knew that this nutcase with the bat could be anyone.

Noise rose up behind him, loud, angry noise, and he picked up his pace even more. Yells, heavy footsteps splashing in the puddles—they were coming from the next street, maybe even from just around the corner. This man wanted his blood, and unless he maintained a sizeable distance from him he would get it. A narrow alleyway appeared up ahead and Harvey quickly darted into it, hoping that his swift change in direction would shake the man off his tail. The alley was thin and cramped, and he was forced to leap over big piles of black bin bags and cardboard boxes, exerting extra effort just to cover more ground. But along he went, regardless, jumping and stepping over about a hundred yards of rubbish and litter, until finally, another main road at the opposite end of the alleyway was in front of him.

He emerged onto the street with a certain amount of confidence, sure that the armed man was a safe distance away. Before he could even begin to think about which way to go next, however, a terrifying roar cut through the night air, reverberating around the desolate shopfronts. Turning his head, Harvey was confronted with a sight that stunned him into paralyses, reducing him into a startled rabbit caught in some dazzling headlights. The tall, menacing figure of his attacker was right there, just a few metres away from him, and in his hands, held high above his head, was an industrial chainsaw, roaring and rattling like crazy. *What? How did he get here so fast? And where did the chainsaw come from?* A million questions raced through Harvey's mind but he didn't have time to ponder any of them, he had to snap himself out of this daze and scarper once again.

With the guttural growl of the chainsaw right behind him Harvey was literally running for his life, but his legs were growing heavy and lead-like and a sinking feeling overcame him, slowing him down even more. He was in serious trouble and he knew it. He was screaming now, calling out for help, but there was no one around to hear it. *Where is everyone? What the hell's going on? How did I end up in this horrifying situation?* He was losing now, losing the battle, and the small gap between him and his determined pursuer was growing even smaller. The evil din of the spinning blade was deafening in his ear, and he could even feel its teeth pinching and snagging on his clothing as the man swung it in wild arcs behind him.

This nightmarish game of cat and mouse went on and on, with Harvey's legs growing heavier, and the rips and snags of the blade growing sharper and closer to his skin, until, with a sickening shriek of petrol and burning tissue, the inevitable happened. A sharp pain sliced down his back, much sharper than the rest, and immobilised him instantly. Tripping over his own feet, he staggered and fell to the pavement, his clothes damp with blood. As the man advanced, looming ominously over his dying body, Harvey looked into his eyes searching for a sign of humanity, but found none. When the blade came down a final time, ripping through his soft flesh, Harvey still had no idea who, or what, was attacking him.

△△△

Another car pulled into the huge car park, a small family inside. A young boy in the back seat had his face pressed up against the window, his parents up in front. It was Saturday, the busiest day for Mapharno City Shopping

Precinct by far, and the lack of parking spaces reflected that. The sky above the precinct's flat roof was clear and blue, and the sun was shining brightly. Sam, the young boy, would usually be moaning and groaning at the prospect of following his parents around while they shopped for mundane items, but today was different. Sam had turned thirteen last week, which meant that he was at last old enough to be left unattended at the giant arcade inside the shopping complex. The Mapharno City Shopping Precinct video game arcade was immense. With close to a hundred machines, it was easily the largest one in the country, and it was also the best because it had *Virtual Vengeance*— the game all the kids at school were talking about.

'We're trusting you here, Sam,' said the boy's mother, once they'd entered the precinct, 'so don't let us down. Don't go disappearing or anything.'

'I won't,' said Sam, eyeing up the dazzling, neon lights of the arcade just up ahead.

The boy's parents weren't especially keen on the idea of leaving him at the arcade to play this game, but its popularity was growing so much that it would've been cruel not to let him play it.

'We'll be about an hour and a half. We'll come in and find you when we're ready to leave,' said his mum, leaning down to give him a peck on the cheek.

And with that, at last, Sam's moment had come. He was finally free to roam the dizzy aisles of the big arcade, with its long rows of flashy, inviting machines. He spent the first five minutes or so in a state of wild hysteria, watching the many paying punters as they hit the joysticks and frantically worked the controls, fluorescent lights of all colours dancing over their faces. When Sam saw a few adults mixed in with the pockets of teenagers, pounding the buttons and shouting at the screens even louder than the adolescents surrounding them, he wondered whether the rumours he'd heard about the game were true; his parents had refused to comment about it either way when he'd asked them, giving him some ambiguous response that'd shed no light on the subject whatsoever. This was unimportant now, though. Nothing but a triviality to his young, excited mind.

Virtual Vengeance was arguably the most addictive video game ever made, and the lines of engrossed players glued to their screens made Sam itch with anticipation as he fished around in his pocket for some money. He'd found a vacant machine over in the corner, sparkling and new, and its allure was pulling him closer to it. Everything about the game was appealing: the graphics, the characters, the setting, the wide range of special moves...the realism. Without wasting anymore time, Sam began frantically stuffing his change into the slot—he was ready to play.

As usual, the punishment wing of Mapharno City Prison was full. The noise was unbearable; screams and wails filled the long, bright room, cries of agony bouncing from the white walls. Some of the nurses and wardens wore earplugs to block out the racket, others just persevered. It was a bizarre and horrid sight: dozens of squirming bodies writhed and jerked about upon the line of white beds, ankles and wrists red raw from the leather restraints. Tears rolled down the stubbled cheeks of some; wet, urine-stained sheets clung to the legs of others. Two small screens were displayed above each inmate's head: one displaying the individual's health statistics, the other displaying his or her "game" in real time.

Now that prisons were another private sector commodity, profits and income were the main priority of most governors, and *Virtual Vengeance* had proven itself to be a major money spinner. The technology had been tricky to produce, and building the expensive shopping precinct and arcade had been a risky venture, but within the first four months the project had completely paid for itself, and then some. A role-playing-game with a difference, *Virtual Vengeance* was a roaring success that solved several different problems simultaneously: it served as a harsh punishment for unruly convicts, helping to keep order in the jails; it alleviated public tension and stress, allowing members of the community to vent some of their anger towards the dregs of society who make their streets unsafe; it served as an effective deterrent for adolescents who were tempted by a life in the criminal underworld, showing them the literal nightmare that would await them if they chose the wrong path in life; and, last but certainly not least, it brought in a huge amount of money for the project organisers, elevating profits to a whole new level.

A nurse and two wardens stood by the bedside of one hysterical inmate, immune and nonreactive to his squeals. It was clear, looking at the screen above his head, that his game was about to end, and so the nurse began to prepare an injection that'd bring him out of his induced coma, while the two wardens got ready to pull the electrodes out from his scalp. Despite the cold, perfunctory manner in which the wardens were going about their duty, they actually felt a little sorry for the inmate thrashing around in front of them on the bed. He was merely a petty criminal, a small-time crook, serving two years for possession of drugs. He'd got into a bit of trouble on the wings, catching the attention of the prison governor, and now here he was, plugged into this brutal machine as punishment.

'Well,' said one of them, leaning over to reach the tangled array of electrodes after the nurse had given him a nod, 'he'll certainly be behaving himself from now on.'

'Huh, yeah, I bet,' said the other, with a sorry shake of his head.

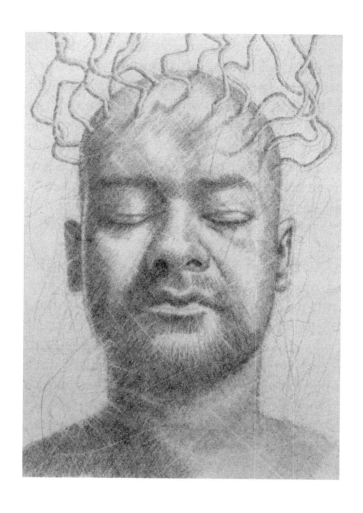

Sam was in his element. He was pounding the buttons, pulling off complex moves and combinations that were causing his character to thrash around in a violent stupor up on the screen. There were various weapons available on this game, but he'd now found his favourite. The baseball bat was fun, but it was nowhere near as good as the chainsaw that he now had. He'd earned it due to an accumulation of points, and it was now helping him to win the game.

As if on cue, just as he was finishing his last move, ending the level, his parents came strolling through the rows of machines, shopping bags in hand. His mother announced that it was time to leave, and Sam, under the addictive spell of the game, opened his mouth to beg for one more go. His father's expression stopped him, however. He had a solemn look on his face that Sam had never really seen before, and it prevented his words from coming out. Sam wondered how much of his game playing he'd seen when he came walking over. Maybe he was a little bit shocked by the ferocity of it all, the violent nature of the gameplay in action?

Not wanting to upset his parents and jeopardise his future chances of revisiting the arcade, Sam pulled himself away from the big machine, already doing mental calculations as to how long it would be before he would get to return here.

'Did you enjoy yourself, dear?' asked his mum, on the way back out towards the car park.

'Yes! Definitely!' replied Sam, skipping along with a spring in his step.

'I hope you're not going to try and copy that game, or anything,' she added, with a touch of concern lacing her voice.

'No, I won't. Of course not.'

'Because I don't really like all of that violence,' she continued. 'If I'm completely honest, I'm only letting you play it because all the other kids seem to be doing so.'

'Don't worry, I wouldn't do anything like that in real life, Mum.'

'Huh, let's hope not,' grumbled his father, 'or it might be you on there one day otherwise.'

Sam, caught somewhat off guard by this unexpected outburst from his father, spun his head round to look at him. 'What?'

His father began to reply but his mum piped up and interrupted, stopping him mid-flow. 'No! We agreed not to, didn't we?'

With a sigh, his father nodded and fell silent, leaving little Sam wondering again about the outlandish rumours he'd heard from his friends at school.

DEADLY
DISPOSSESSION

He made a kind decision, a very noble one

It was a hard thing to do, because he loved his son

Letting go wasn't easy, and he started to crack

That's the reason why, he wanted the bloody thing back!

PART 1

It's Friday night. The sound of distant partying makes its way through my apartment window, and into my cluttered living room. Drunken laughter and boozy banter can be heard down on the street two floors below, as groups of drinkers stagger from one pub to the next. My night has no such enjoyment in store, however. My night, the night of Eric Harris, is going to be far from enjoyable.

Old, flaking cardboard boxes surround me as I sit on the floor, trying to sort through the endless clutter that I've brought back from my parents' house. It's been a month since the accident, and I've hardly made any progress at all in clearing out the old family home. The shock, the pain, the trauma, the sudden loneliness... it's all just too much.

All four of us had been in the car that night: me, my wife, and both of my parents. We were on our way back from a weekend break. It was only a cheap, all-inclusive deal at some small hotel on the coast, but we all enjoyed ourselves. It was late on Sunday night and I was driving back. Everyone else was dozing in the car, and I was trying my best not to do the same as I sped along down the motorway. I've been wondering whether I was actually asleep too when the car in the next lane lost control and skidded into us, because I can remember so little about it. There was a mighty thump against the door as we collided, that I recall, but before that everything's kind of hazy. After that awful thump it was all screeching tarmac and shattered glass, bits of plastic dashboard flying through the air. The tormenting part of it all, the bit that nags away at my mind the most, is the fact that my wife, mother, and father all survived that initial impact; it was the oncoming traffic from behind that killed them.

The car was compressed to half its size. I only managed to survive due to the angle that the cars hit us. The doctors said I was lucky. Looking around me tonight, alone in the silence of the empty flat, I have to say that I beg to differ. The driver who caused the accident didn't hang around, and the eye- witness accounts are all very sketchy and unspecific. The most the police have to go on is that the car was green, possibly a hatchback. Nothing too promising.

It's kind of ironic that I was the one who survived that night, considering my chequered medical history. I'm certainly no stranger to hospitals. In fact, I've pretty much been in and out of them all my life. By the time I was twelve years old I'd already spent more time in hospitals than an average person does in their lifetime. It's my heart, you see. Well, I suppose I should say it *was* my heart. I underwent heart surgery at that tender age, after struggling through my childhood years with serious problems and complications. The doctors said that heart transplantation was my only option, and the ten-inch scar across my chest is a constant reminder of that. Nowadays I pretty much have a clean bill of health, but I still can't help seeing the irony of me surviving when everyone else died.

So here I am, alone, picking up the pieces of my shattered life. I'm burdened with the daunting task of clearing out my parents' old house before putting it up for sale; hopefully, after that, I can attempt to build a new life for myself. If I feel strong enough, that is. I sigh with despair, like a balloon deflating. Either side of me I've got piles of old letters, bills, video tapes, DVD's, CD's, plates, clothes, ornaments, and countless other stuff that's been sitting up in a loft gathering dust for the last decade or so. A pile of paper sleeves catches my eye, and I'm drawn towards them. I can tell without even touching them that they're full of old family photos, and I also know that if I start flicking through them all I'm going to spend at least a couple of hours doing so, and won't get any work done.
What the hell, I mutter.

△△△

The photos do nothing to ease the pain. Every single one of them is simply a grim reminder of what I once had—of what I've lost. Bent, yellowed pictures from years ago pass through my fingers, pictures that I'd long forgotten about, stages of my life lost to the sands of time. Strange haircuts leap out at me from faded snapshots in locations I don't recognise, outdated clothing makes me cringe and tingle with embarrassment even though there's nobody else here to see it.

They don't all feature me, of course. A thick stack of them are from my parents' wedding, and there are countless others of distant relatives I've never even met before. I find myself looking for more pictures of me and my mother together; something that I can keep in my wallet, maybe. An old Polaroid sticks out from the pack and I pick it up. It's a holiday photo. I remember this one well; it was taken in Tenerife. I was twelve years old, and my father had treated us all to a vacation after the stress we'd been through after my operation. There's a big rock formation in the centre of the page and I'm standing on it, my mother looking up at me with a proud look in her eye. The haze of an afternoon sun simmers behind us, leading out towards the sea. How I wish I could morph myself into the picture, jump back into that carefree moment in the warm sun, somehow. Things were far from perfect back then, but they were a hell of a lot better than this. I carefully place it down on the floor beside me, and continue browsing.

A picnic photo catches my eye this time, and this one also has both me and my mother in it. The two of us are sitting on a blanket in a park somewhere, a selection of plates, cups, and containers laid out around us. My father probably took the photograph, as I can see an extra pair of shoes on the grass in front of us. I look slightly older in this one; a couple of years, maybe. Studying the picture closely, it's clear that we were not the only ones in the mood for a picnic that day, as several other people are visible in the background. A trio of young students are sat to the left of us, beer cans in hand, an elderly couple to the right, and off in the background a lone man is sitting on a bench.

A strange sensation hits me when I see this man, a kind of unexplained familiarity. Studying this man in the background of the old photo, I feel as though I've seen him before. This in itself would've been enough to disturb me somewhat, but my discomfort is heightened even further by the fact that the recognition feels recent, like I've seen him somewhere else within the last few minutes. His features are fresh in my mind. He has an odd look about him. His face is grey and pasty, and a thick pair of spectacles circle his beady eyes like round frames. Mousy white hair covers his head.

A thought enters my head. It's a stupid thought, ridiculous even, but I can't help but listen to it. I go back to the previous photo, the one of me climbing the rock formation. I don't fully know why I'm doing it, it's more of a subconscious impulse, as if a deeper part of my mind knows something that I don't. This impulse obviously holds some merit, however, because a second later I see him. He's there, in the background of the first photo, this time perched on a rocky wall instead of a bench. My blood runs cold with a creepy, eerie terror. I compare the two photos, checking the face a few times, hoping dearly that I'm wrong. But my hope is short lived because there is simply no mistaking it—it's the same man.

My fingers tremble and the two photographs drop to the floor. The air in my living room feels cold all of a sudden; tense. It can't be right, it just can't be. The two photos were taken years apart in completely different parts of the world, so how could this random stranger be in the background of both of them? *It's the stress*, I tell myself, getting up to go and make a drink. This is, of course, the rational explanation, but as I wait in the kitchen for the kettle to boil I'm neither reassured nor convinced.

△△△

The hot tea I've just brewed tastes good, and I welcome the warmth of it. Feeling a little calmer, I start flicking through the old photos again, and this time I'm specifically looking for the white-haired man. There are dozens of pictures but I patiently sift through them, curious to see if I can find any more with him in them. Half an hour passes with no result. A multitude of pictures come out of the boxes, but he's nowhere to be seen in any of them.

It takes another forty minutes of searching before his face stares up at me again from one of the glossy surfaces, but this time it's clearer than ever.

This photo's pretty recent, and sharper, with more definition. It can't be more than two years old. Me and my ex-wife are smiling at the camera, sitting down in a restaurant across town that used to be our favourite. I remember the night well. This man, this spectacled man, he's sitting over on a table behind us, alone. He's looking away from the camera, his jaw set tight. This one really puts the hook in me, because it's so close to home. The restaurant is less than a mile away from my apartment, less than a mile away from where I sit right now. I look closely at this one; *real* close. Everything about him is strange: the black glasses, the bushy eyebrows hanging over the top, the slate-grey skin, the brown suit that looks as though it's been worn a million times. A familiarity hits me again, but this time it's different. This time I get a feeling that I've actually spoken to this man at some point, interacted with him in some way. Now that I can see him clearly like this, his face is known to me, as though he's played a part in the structure of my life somehow.

I put this photograph with the other two, then continue searching.

Another hour passes by as I go through the boxes, flicking through every image I can find. A school photo works its way to the top of the pile I'm looking at, and a tremor runs through me as I look down at the printed image. It's a secondary school, end-of-year, class picture, and thirty or so students are all lined up, including me. A handful of teachers stand either side of us, arranged neatly into the composition. A mop of silver-white hair draws my eyes to it like a beacon, and now, I realise, I have a name to put to the face.

Mr Crisp. The name springs up out of nowhere, like it's been waiting impatiently for an opportunity to rise to the surface of my mind for the last couple of hours. Mr Crisp the supply teacher. How did I not realise this straight away? How did I not remember that face? That hair? He used to come into the school and teach us when others teachers were off sick, filling time by handing out crossword puzzles and word searches to twenty or so uninterested kids. He was as eccentric as they come, always erratic and on edge.

This revelation only deepens the whole mystery, though. Why is an old school teacher of mine lurking in the background of several photographs that've been sitting in my parents' loft for years on end? It's all too much for my tired, fragile head to take, and I wince as I look up at the clock on the wall and see how late it is. My bed is calling me, and I'm calling it. This riddle needs a refreshed mind to solve it, I decide, so I stand up and go to the bathroom to brush my teeth.

Standing in front of the mirror, I run through the possibilities. It simply wouldn't be feasible to put all of this down to a simple, innocent coincidence, that much is true, I acknowledge to myself. With this option lost to me, I turn to the tenuous hope that this whole entire fiasco might just be some fatigue-induced hallucination, something that'll cease to exist when I open my eyes in the morning. The idea is pleasant and sooth-ing, and I cling to it dearly.

PART 2

The last two days have been torturous. Some of the boxes have been cleared away now, but the pile of photos sit on my living room table, silently taunting me every minute of every hour. I've been thinking about reporting the issue to the police, but the more I consider it the more futile it seems. No crime has been committed, and all I have are some old pictures. The uncomfortable scenarios that run through my head are enough to put me off going to the station: incredulous stares from overworked officers; smirks and giggles as I pull out the old, faded photos of me as a child; the embarrassment of walking out after being told there's nothing that they can do. The whole thing is too flimsy for the authorities to deal with, but on the other hand, it's too serious for me to ignore.

The only thing I really have to go on is the name. I figure there can't be that many people around with a surname like Crisp, so perhaps I can track him down on my own somehow. The local registry office, the public library, the employee records at my old school... all of these things are running through my head as I stuff the selected pack of photos in my bag and walk out the door, determined to find some answers.

Walking down the street makes me nervous. I feel exposed; naked, almost. The invisible weight of eyes and stares press down on me, and I hold onto my bag as though it's a comfort blanket. There's a bus that goes directly to the council offices and I wait at the stop by the end of the road, glancing around me. The handful of commuters waiting at the bus stop keep their distance from me, and people walking past veer off towards the curb to avoid getting too close. It's at this precise moment that I realise how troubled and disturbed I must look, how noticeable and visible my stress must be to those in my close vicinity. I find myself wondering how I would react if I were to see myself in this way as a passer-by.

The bus comes rolling by after a few minutes, and the small crowd along the pavement try their best to get themselves lined up with the doors so that they can get on first. I'm the last to get on, and I awkwardly grab hold of the door rail and begin to heave myself up onto the big step. I'm halfway on the bus when I stop, frozen mid-stride, half my body hanging out of the big automatic doors. A strange colour catches my eye and I'm drawn to it, looking over towards it while I balance on the edge of the step. The colour is brown, a sickly shade of brown, and it comes from a blazer a man is wearing on the corner of the street. There's something about the blazer that demands my attention, some oddity, and then, when I see the grey mop of hair flapping around above it, I realise exactly what, or who, I'm looking at.

The loud, impatient voice of the bus driver snaps me out of my frightened daze, and I'm then forced to make a split-second decision to either step onto the bus and drive away in relative safety, or step off the bus and confront this apparition-like figure that stands fifty yards away from me on the corner of the road. Deep down, I know what I have to do. I jump off the bus and let it pull away, the angry, disgruntled faces of the passengers whizzing past me in a blur as it accelerates down the road, leaving me alone to face my demon.

Without a single word from either one of us we draw closer to each other, walking through the thick cloud of exhaust fumes the bus left in its wake. Our eyes are locked in a tense, mutual understanding; our bodies move in unison. Each second feels like a year as we edge towards one another, and I take in everything I can about him. In the flesh Mr Crisp looks even creepier. There's a desperation lurking under the surface of his grey skin, a beseeching expression carved across his weathered features. His presence is intimidating but not in an aggressive sense, rather an eccentric one; his posture and demeanour paints a picture of imbalance and unpredictability. He looks at me not with hate but with longing, behaving in the manner of someone meeting a long-lost relative they haven't seen in a while.

'Alex,' he whispers, coming to a gentle halt before me on the pavement.

It takes a few moments for the name to register with me, as I'm trembling all over and my head is a jittery ball of fuzz. Just as I'm about to correct him, however, he leans forward ever so slightly and continues, his voice raspy and high-pitched.

'I'm so glad you've remembered, so glad you're here again. Please come with me. There are so many things we need to discuss.'

'I'm not going anywhere with you,' I cry. 'You're going to tell me what the hell's going on, and you're going to do it right now! Right here!'

My outburst surprises him and he seems to switch gears, the tone and pitch of his voice altering as though he's now talking to someone completely different.

'Please come with me,' he says, this time with more calculation and control. 'I'll explain everything.'

'Who are you? Why have you been following me?'

'I'm... an old friend. An old friend of your parents.'

The mention of my parents arouses a fresh

burst of emotion and I yell at him again, causing a couple of pedestrians across the road to turn their heads.

'An old friend of my parents? I've never even —'

Reaching into his blazer pocket he pulls out a card, throwing me off kilter for a second and cutting off my words. He passes it over to me and I hesitantly take it, studying its yellowed antiquity. It's an old thank you card with an outdated design, but I instantly recognise the handwriting inside. It's my mother's writing; the curves and strokes leap out at me from the stained paper. I look up at Mr Crisp with a steely expression, demanding some kind of explanation.

'Just read it, and you'll see that you can trust me,' he says. I read the card.

Dear Mr Crisp, we could never thank you enough for what you have done, but please just know that we are forever in your debt for your kindness. We can only envy your warmth and generosity. If there's anything we can do for you, just let us know.

I still have no clear idea of what's going on, but after reading these words I feel as though I should at least hear Mr Crisp out and listen to what he has to say. I hand the card back to him, loosening up slightly.

'Let's get away from here,' he says. 'We're

making a scene.'

Taking a deep breath, I slowly nod and concede. We walk around the corner and away from the main road, leaving the noisy traffic behind us.

△△△

I'm sitting in the passenger seat of Mr Crisp's car as he navigates the roads. There's a musty smell to the interior, but it looks fairly clean and tidy. A silence lingers between us, and I focus most of my attention on memorising the route we're taking.

He drives the way you'd expect an elderly man to drive: obeying every speed limit, indicating at every turn, stopping for every red light, etc. I feel fairly safe in the car with him, sensing no risk of any kind of traffic collision. Now and again, as he changes gears and steers the old car around corners, I surreptitiously study him from the corner of my eye. Judging by the deep creases in his skin and the frailty of his limbs, I reckon he must be in his late sixties at least.

We eventually turn into a quiet, leafy street, with neat-looking houses lining each side. With careful concentration he maneuvers the car onto a brick driveway, then finally cuts the engine.

'Here we are,' he says, smiling at me warmly through his thick black glasses.

After getting out of the car I look around, checking my surroundings for anything suspicious. Nothing seems amiss. A gentle gust of breeze blows leaves across the innocent-looking street, and the only real activity I see is a black cat stretching its arms and legs as it lays across a patch of grass. But despite the lack of any kind of visible threat, my pulse still quickens as I follow Mr Crisp to the front door. It's too late to back out now, however, so I simply reassure myself by acknowledging the fact that I could physically overcome this man if I really needed to.

The house is decorated and furnished but it has an empty feel to it, and I can instantly tell that Mr Crisp lives alone. A cushioned sofa sits in the corner of the living room with various shelves, wooden chairs, and ornaments positioned here and there. Everything I see has a dated look to it.

'Please make yourself at home,' he says, waving an arm towards the old sofa. 'Would you like a drink?'

'No thanks,' I reply.

Thankfully, Mr Crisp keeps his distance, pulling up one of the wooden chairs to sit on. 'It must feel good to be back, does it not?'

'What?' I reply, startled.

An embarrassed look crosses Mr Crisp's face, and he corrects himself. 'Oh, nothing, erm...look, why don't we—'

'Why don't you start by telling me why you've been following me?' I interrupt. 'Why are you present in some of my family photos?'

'What photos, Alex?'

'What photos?!'

My hands are shaking as they fumble around inside my bag, but I eventually locate the paper sleeve and throw it onto his lap.

'Here! *These* photos!'

A warm smile appears on his face as he flicks through them, and it's only then that I realise he's addressed me by a different name again. Just as I'm about to ask him why, however, he starts muttering to himself.

'Oh, the memories. So many years ago now.'

'What do you mean? Why were you even there in the first place?!' I scream. I'm on the verge of losing it. The stress of the last couple of days, as well as the last few weeks, wells up inside of me, looking for an outlet. 'And why do you keep on calling me Alex?'

A look of concern crosses the old man's face, but only for a second. 'Let me show you something...' His voice trails off before any name is uttered, but then he continues: '...that'll make everything fall into place.'

He rises from the wooden chair and walks towards the door, beckoning me to follow. I do so, rising from the sofa and gingerly walking across the room. We go along the downstairs hallway, all the way to the staircase. The stairs creak under our weight as we both climb them, Mr Crisp leading the way. The walls are lined with beige wallpaper, with faded floral patterns printed across it; it makes me feel dizzy as it skims past in my peripheral vision.

We make it to the upstairs landing, and he comes to a halt outside one of the bedrooms. The door is closed.

'Come on in,' he says, pushing the door handle down with one hand and adjusting his glasses with the other.

A strange smell hits my nose as the door opens. It's a dusty, stagnant smell, but there's something else there as well. *Dirt. Soil, maybe.* The curtains are drawn, but sunlight penetrates through an inch- wide gap, giving my eyes just enough light to adjust to.

After a moment or two I realise that I'm standing in a child's bedroom. Curled, dog-eared posters hang from the walls with bits of tape, and an array of comic books and magazines litter the floor. It looks to me like a boy's room, but everything is faded and covered in a thin layer of dust. Standing there, surrounded by these delicate, untouched items, I actually feel as though I'm in a museum rather than a child's bedroom, and my body stiffens with fear and uncertainty. Mr Crisp moves around the room and I watch him, noticing the way he carefully steps over the old books and magazines as though they're sacred items.

He finally stops by a bed in the corner. It's a small, single bed with a thin duvet; it's too dark to make out the exact colour. There's not much light in this corner of the room so it takes my eyes another few seconds to focus properly, but when they do I let out a startled cry and take a step back. To my astonishment, a small form is visible under the bedcovers, a figure laid on its back. The arms and legs look skinny; withered, even.

'Who...*is* that?'

Through the dingy murk of the room, I see Mr Crisp's lips curl up into a loving, adoring smile.

'It's you Alex, my boy! It's you! You just need to...' His gaze drops down a notch, as though he's

staring at my chest. '...get back in there.'

The room begins to spin and breath around me as I realise who it is on the bed. Raising my hand to my chest, I feel the lump of my scar running down towards my abdomen, the pink raised tissue that formed after my heart transplant all those years ago. I'd been twelve at the time, and my donor had been roughly the same age.

Movement from the shadows snaps me out of my nightmarish train of thought, and I look up to see Mr Crisp pulling back the covers on the old bed, exposing the skeletal form underneath. Dried skin clings to the arrangement of splintered bones, wrapping tightly around them like scraps of shiny leather, the only exception being the parts of the broken rib cage that stick out and reach for the ceiling. Further up the bed a skull rests on the pillow, two black sockets sunk deep into it. The mattress cover is sprinkled with clumps of some kind of dark substance, presumably soil from the boy's grave.

Slowly but surely, I'm backing away from the bed, trying to gain some distance from Mr Crisp so that I can reach the door without him getting to me first. I manage about three steps before he notices what I'm doing.

'Come on now, Alex. Let's just get everything back in place, and things can go back to normal.'

'Get back! Stay away from me!'

He's edging towards me now, walking around the bed.

'I know that you can hear me, Alex. Don't let him control you.'

A reflection flashes up from where he's standing, caused by the beam of sunlight coming through the crack in the curtains. Mr Crisp's hand then rises up to reveal a surgical scalpel blade, light and razor sharp. I scramble for the door in a frenzy, feeling the delicate pages of old comic books rip and tear under my feet as I go. I'm out of the room in no time, leaping back down the staircase two steps at a time. The front door comes into view just as Mr Crisp's stumbling footsteps rise up behind me, and I lunge for it and yank down the handle. Relief washes over me like a cool, welcome breeze as it swings open, and I throw myself out onto the sunny driveway. I'm barely halfway across it when I hear Mr Crisp's nasal voice from behind me, it's raspy screech sending my hairs up on end.

'Be strong, Alex! Don't let him take you away from me!'

I need to see how close he is, so I turn my head and have a look. He's standing right there in the doorway, silvery hair ruffled and askew. His scrawny hand still clutches the chrome scalpel. There's a wild, possessed look about him, and in this fraction of a second, as I look back at him over my shoulder and gaze into those tormented, panicked eyes, I suddenly see him as a victim. I see the deluded, deranged soul that lurks within him, the man who lost his son, the man who lost his grip, the man who lost his sanity, the man who became so lonely and desperate he committed his entire life to following me around, even going as far as some-how getting a part-time job at a school I used to attend. But the thing is, the real truth of the matter, is that he hasn't actually been following *me* around all these years, he's been following this heart that thumps away in my chest, the last remaining piece of his beloved son.

Seeing him in this sympathetic light alters my view of him, but it doesn't make him any less dangerous, so I continue running across the driveway towards the road. As I do so, I see one last thing that causes the remaining pieces of this twisted puzzle to fall into place.

The car is still there in front of the house, Mr Crisp's car, and there's a huge dent in the off-side wing. I'd failed to notice it earlier, but it's there, big and deep. Another thing I'd failed to notice was the actual colour of the car—or the significance of its colour. *Mr Crisp's car is green.* This fact consciously registers with me for the first time as I'm halfway across the drive, mid-stride. The official police report of the car accident that killed my family included a description of a green car. I need no further clues to convince me that Mr Crisp was the one who ran us all off the road that night, no further evidence is needed, but it comes, anyway.

A broken streak of red paint runs along the inside of the dent. My old car, the car I was driving on the night of the accident, was this same shade of red.

My legs ache due to the vicious pace at which I'm sprinting, but I don't slow down, not one bit. There's a main road not far up ahead in the direction that I'm heading, I remember it on the way here. My only plan is to flag down a police car, maybe. Beyond that, I'm literally running wild, concentrating only on widening the distance between me and the house at any cost.

Heads turn in the street as I run, curtains twitch behind windows, lampposts and garden gates whizz past me in a blur. I stop for nothing, ignoring small alleyways and side roads, leaping over curbs and drain covers like they're not even there.

This goes on for several minutes, running through the suburban streets, but then, out of nowhere, I'm overcome with a sudden sensation of flying. It's completely unexpected and bizarre. My legs actually leave the floor, and a vast blue sky takes over my field of vision. For the briefest of seconds it seems as though some kind of bird has swooped down and lifted me into the air, but then the illusion shatters when I feel my body drop and smash down onto rough tarmac. The towering bulk of a double- decker bus then looms over me, the frightening sight punctuated by the sickening sound of screeching brake discs. A scream and a gasp rises up from somewhere, then heads and faces appear around me in a circle as I look up in a daze. Phones are pressed against ears, and details are exchanged.

Seconds pass, then minutes, then, very

gradually, the distant sound of sirens fills the air. I'm aware of all of this, but only dimly, and by the time the ambulance arrives I feel completely detached from my surroundings.

△△△

Bright lights pass over me, the fluorescent glare glowing behind my closed eyelids. When I eventually open my eyes I see the ceiling panels of a hospital corridor, accompanied by the bleeping sounds of medical equipment around my head. Masked nurses chatter to each other as they push me along on the stretcher.

I've been in many hospitals over the years, but this time it feels different; this time feels like the last time. I feel separated from everything, including my body, sinking down into a black hole. I have one last thing to say to the world, however. There's one last piece of information that I need to share, and I try hard to fight against the deep fatigue that's pushing me down so that I can spit it out.

Even the simple task of opening my mouth takes a herculean effort of willpower and determination, though. My lips are heavier than lead, and my tongue feels like a sleeping boulder at the bottom of some deep ocean. I groan and moan, cough and splutter, frantically trying to put a sentence together so that I can inform the nurses that a crazed, deranged man is on the loose and that the police need to be called immediately. But the words won't come, only a long series of incomprehensible gurgling sounds, and to make matters worse, after a few moments one of the nurses interprets my noises as a call for some kind of pain relief, and she lowers a big plastic mask over my face which blasts me with gas and air. Everything around me turns into blurred patches of colour, the colours merging and swirling together, and then, as I sink lower and lower, the colours fade and disintegrate into nothing.

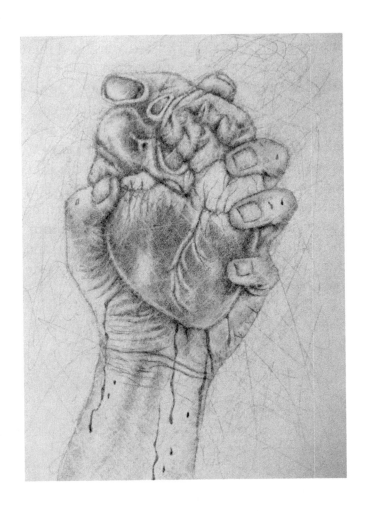

196

PART 3

D own near the ground floor entrance of the hospital, a small family waits in anticipation. When the elevator pings and the doors slide open, they all clasp their hands tightly around each other, and the mother begins to weep. A wheelchair emerges from the lift, pushed along by a nurse, and perched on the seat is their beloved relative, a young man recovering from his major operation.

The last few months have been hard for the family, especially the parents. With a shortage of donors in the area it began to seem like their son would never get a new heart, but a recent fatal traffic collision involving a bus and a pedestrian created a change of circumstance for them. Finally, after waiting for so long, their son had been given the transplant that he'd needed.

A brief exchange is made between the nurse and the family: reminders about medication to be taken, information about dates and times of follow-up appointments, and then final pleasantries and farewells.

Outside in the car park they all help him to

get into the car, then fold up the wheelchair and put it into the boot. Two minutes later the car pulls out of the hospital and accelerates down the road, joining the stream of traffic. The atmosphere in the car is happy and joyous, the conversations filled with optimistic plans for the future. They are all lost in the emotional moment; so lost, in fact, that no one notices the car that's tailing them, mirroring their every turn. So engrossed are they in this happy, emotional moment that not one of them notices this green car with the dent in the wing, and the crazed, bespectacled man hunched over the steering wheel.

NOSTALGIA

She went out on a drug binge, one she couldn't afford
Then found herself bedbound, stuck in a hospital ward
At first she flipped and panicked, fighting with all her might
But then she saw the doctor, and he wished her goodnight

Dr Clingwill went from bed to bed, checking the patients' drips and dressings. The small ward was calm and quiet apart from the bleeps and hums of the machines, and the gentle rattling of the windows from a breeze outside. He was almost done for the day, his duties nearly completed, there were just some final tasks to be taken care of before he could leave and make his way home to the other side of Rachton.

A bandage had begun to peel away from an elderly man's shoulder and he stuck it back down with some surgical tape, his ocean-blue eyes full of focus and intensity as he did so. Another patient on an adjacent bed was dribbling from the side of his mouth and he leaned over to him and wiped it clean, his touch delicate and precise.

From certain angles Dr Clingwill could be described as handsome, in a traditional, perhaps old-fashioned sense. With his white jacket and stethoscope, his combed brown hair and smooth face, he certainly looked the part. The only thing that tainted his clean image was the fact that he maybe tried too hard to look tidy and presentable, his manicured look giving off a sense of desperation and effort to the observant viewer. His parted hair had an unnatural tint to it, the after-effect of some off-the-shelf dye, and his pearly-white teeth were obviously caps.

In terms of work ethic, though, the man was exemplary in every way. A sick day was an alien concept, lateness didn't exist, and professionalism oozed from his every pore. The medical profession ran through his veins and flowed through his blood, and nobody could take that away from him.

Once he was satisfied that his ward was in order and his patients were in a good condition, he washed his hands at a sink by the wall and then made his way over to his office on the same floor of the hospital. Not one single worker passed him on the way, no nurses or surgeons brushing past him along the corridors, but this was all simply a testament to his excellent work and dedication. While he was on the job, nobody else was needed—that's how he saw it, anyway.

It took him twenty minutes or so to write up his notes. Sitting there behind his desk—the desk that'd been in the same spot for longer than he cared to remember—he wrote a brief report for each one of the bed-bound patients, cutting no corners with any of the details or figures. Once they were done, he filed the papers away in a filing cabinet behind him and gathered his personal belongings together, finally allowing himself to end his shift.

After climbing into a rather dated-looking car, Clingwill inserted a plastic cassette tape into the stereo and pulled out of the hospital grounds, locking a security gate behind him. The huge hospital building shrunk and receded in the rear-view mirror as he accelerated away from the complex, its dark brickwork and black guttering merging together in the distance.

Passing motorists turned their heads as the doctor cruised along the main roads of the town, the automobile's retro shape and design catching most people's attention. Clingwill seemed oblivious to this, however; sat upright in the driver's seat with his manicured hands gripping the wheel, he was somewhere else entirely, lost in the sounds of a bygone decade as the tape played.

It didn't take that long for him to get home, around forty minutes or so, and when he reached his leafy street he pulled up on his driveway and killed the engine. Trudging across the stones, he made his way to the front door. He knew that his wife would be at home, and after fumbling around with his keys for a while, working the stiff lock, he poked his head around the frame and called her name.

'Katherine?'

A faint reply came from the living room, and so he then proceeded to hang up his coat and take his shoes off in the hallway, his presence in the house declared. Running a hand through his immaculate hair, he breathed a satisfied sigh of relief at having completed another day.

The doctor's home was as neat and organised as his office, and his wife, Katherine, was sitting in her usual place on the cream sofa, her face creased in concentration as she pondered some crossword puzzle on her lap. Clingwill walked over and sat next to her, planting a kiss on her cheek, before asking her about her day.

The two of them lived a quiet life together, but they were happy. They'd been through some ups and downs in recent times, what with Clingwill's job, but they'd fought through them all and now, after a lot of hard work and determination, arranging and rearranging, things were back to how they were. By eight o' clock the two of them were huddled together, engrossed in a film flashing out of the chunky TV set, a decades-old mystery drama which they'd both seen more than once, lost in the grainy, familiar scenes.

$$\triangle\triangle\triangle$$

Zoe was staggering along the pavement, her

steps erratic and sloppy. She'd just emerged from the dingy tower block behind her in the distance, after overindulging once again with her shady group of acquaintances. Life was uncertain right now for young Zoe. A year ago her parents had kicked her out of the family home for quitting college and smoking drugs in the house, and since then things had gone from bad to worse. Her occasional, social drug use had swiftly turned into a regular habit, and the mild homegrown cannabis had progressed into stronger stuff like MDMA and cocaine. She'd turned into something of a lost soul, sleeping on sofas and floors, no real direction to her life, and the few decent friends she once had now avoided her and didn't answer her calls, tired of lending her money and not getting it back.

Funding this habit of hers was obviously a continuous problem, and she'd run up a number of debts with several people. With twice as many enemies as friends she should have been slowing down, but on the contrary her recklessness seemed to be escalating. Tonight, she'd settled one of her smaller debts by dropping to her knees in front of a particularly horny dealer, hence the reason she'd gotten her fix despite having an empty purse.

The problem she faced now was finding a place to crash for the night, but she knew someone who would probably let her sleep at their flat as long as she shared her packet with them, and so it was there that she was headed. Progress was slow, though. Teeth grinding from the MDMA, nose blocked from the lines she'd sniffed from the coffee table up in the apartment block, the terrain in front of her was a dark blur punctuated by streaks of orange street lighting, all swirling in an unfocused whirlpool in front of her dilated pupils. Her legs felt like thin slices of jelly, wobbling and struggling to support her weight, and after bumping into a lamppost she finally buckled and fell across a grass verge that was damp with cold dew drops and patches of urine. She was conscious, but only just, dimly aware of the succession of car headlights tearing past on the main road a short distance away. When one of the cars stopped, apparently to see if she was OK and check on her, she felt as though she were sinking down into the wet mud and grass, slipping away into a chemical haze. The last thing she heard before oblivion were the words: 'Let's get you to safety...' before her eyelids dropped shut like lead weights.

△△△

When her eyelids finally opened again it

was no longer dark, nor was she outside. She was staring up at a high ceiling with rows of long lights positioned in straight lines, the plastic casings yellowed and cracked with age. It took a long time for her eyes to adjust to her new surroundings, and even then things were still fuzzy and hazy around the edges, as though she were viewing things through a fish-eye lens.

She was stretched out upon a bed, that much she could tell. The bed was soft but not too soft, with a wafer-thin sheet covering her tender body which she could just make out in her lower peripheral vision. I'm in a hospital! Oh, no! What happened? What did I do last night? Her groggy mind worked itself into a frenzy trying to recall the events of the previous evening, but all it could come up with was vague snapshots of drinking and bingeing in some rundown apartment somewhere.

She tried to get up, but couldn't. An invisible force pinned her body to the bed like a ten-tonne weight, and this horrible realisation caused panic to ripple through her. She then tried to scream but found that her voice wouldn't work, either, no matter how much she strained to make a noise. In fact, the most she could do in terms of bodily function was turn her head left and right by about an inch on both sides, and so she did this continuously, trying to take in as much of the strange room as possible. A large window space to her right-hand-side revealed a cloudy sky with a line of treetops poking their heads above the sill; over to her left, the square outline of another bed was visible, with a scrawny foot hanging out from under the edge of the sheets; on the other side of the room, in front of her, was a closed door. The air was stagnant, dusty and, apart from a series of dull bleeps coming from somewhere behind her, quiet. OK, calm down. Keep calm. I probably just passed out last night, or something. I was drinking, taking things. A nurse will be along in a minute, and they'll tell me exactly what happened.

With focus and willpower she forced herself to relax and close her eyes again, while she waited for a staff member to come along.

Zoe was pulled out of a light sleep by the sound of a creaky door hinge. She was dimly aware of a tall man entering the room, sheathed in white, his lean figure moving its way towards her bed. As she regained consciousness again she was greeted to the sight of two piercing blue eyes looking down at her lovingly, the warm gaze instantly putting her panicked mind at ease. A doctor was here, at her side with a clipboard clutched in his left hand, and a faint smile creased the sides of her mouth in relief.

'You're awake,' the man said, with a healthy

dose of compassion in his voice. 'I was starting to get a little bit worried about you.'

'Wherrr...Wherrr...am...,' Zoe wheezed.

'You're in an intensive care ward, my dear. You were in a terrible state last night, intoxicated and dehydrated to a dangerous level, and you were brought in here after collapsing in the street. Don't worry, though,' he winked, 'I've dosed you up with vitamins, and your drip is slowly re-hydrating you.'

The doctor looked down towards her arm as he said this, and for the first time Zoe realised that a plastic tube was indeed attached to the inside of her elbow. She couldn't turn her head enough to see it, but she could feel it there as a dull sensation against her skin.

There was a million things she wanted to say to the doctor now that he was there with her. She wanted to ask him what hospital she was in, whether anybody had been informed of her admission, and how long she'd be there for, but...she couldn't. The strange paralysis that'd taken over her body was still there, pinning her down to the mattress, preventing even her vocal chords from working properly. She also wanted to ask him why she felt so immobilised, so incapacitated, but all she could manage to do was make a few incoherent gurgling noises.

'Don't you worry about a thing,' said the doctor, noticing her inner struggle. 'You're in safe hands; everybody gets the best treatment

209

in my ward.'

'Uurrrgghhh...'

'Get some rest, you need it,' he said, finally turning away from her to tend to other patients.

Zoe was screaming inside, yelling at him not to leave her, but nothing except a series of groans and grunts came out of her chapped lips. She lay there, wriggling and squirming again like a worm on a hook, while the doctor paced around just outside of her view, whistling and scribbling notes on his clipboard.

ΔΔΔ

'See you tonight, dear!' shouted Dr Clingwill, stepping out of his front door and strolling towards his car. While the old engine was warming up, rattling away on the driveway, he checked his dyed hair in the rear-view mirror and adjusted his tie. Some presenter was harping on about a rise in missing persons on the radio, a few tramps and tearaways disappearing, so he pushed the cassette tape back in and replaced the irritating noise with nostalgic music. Once the car's angry noises and grumbles had died down, he reversed out onto the road and pulled away.

The first port of call for Clingwill on this particular morning was the chemist, where the owners knew him by face and by name.

'Ah, hello Doctor!' said a portly man behind the counter as he walked in.

'I'm here to pick up my order,' said Clingwill, beaming his warm, clean smile.

'Yes, of course,' replied the man, searching behind him for a white paper bag with the relevant label. 'How's things over at the practice?'

'Very well, thank you. Just fine.'

The chemist nodded and smiled at Clingwill's brief reply, and left it at that. He felt rather sorry for the doctor, as did a lot of people around town. The closing of the old hospital had been devastating for him, costing him his job, and without being offered a position at the new, grand, Rachton State Hospital, he'd been forced to open up a private general practice in a different borough somewhere. This upturning of his life couldn't of happened at a worse time, either, what with his wife's health issues back then.

'Here are your supplies, Doctor,' he said, placing the bag on the counter. 'I'm glad things are going well again.'

'Have a wonderful day,' grinned Clingwill, playfully, his clean-shaven mouth curling up into a humble grin.

With a courteous nod he turned and left,

the bag of medicine dangling from his moisturised hand.

The signs and notices by the side of the road were invisible to Clingwill as he turned right into the small lane. The words "Trespassers will be prosecuted" existed, but at the same time didn't exist. The colours and letters flashed before his eyes, but his brain swept them away some place hidden. The steel notices existed in some realm somewhere, some other dimension, but not the realm of his focused, conscious mind. The same held true for the tall barbed wire fence and the iron gates that he unlocked everyday upon entering the hospital grounds: he knew that they were there, existing somewhere in solid form, but he refused to acknowledge them as part of his world. From Clingwill's point of view the entrance to the hospital looked just as it did during the peak of his career, back when everything was OK.

As soon as he'd absently opened the big gate and entered the grounds, the original, council-issued padlock snapped and disposed of long ago, he drove down the long, overgrown road towards the staff car park. He had no trouble finding a parking space, what with the entire lot being a messy, weed-ridden, pothole-covered patch of abandoned tarmac, and after switching off the engine and gathering his bags he stepped out of the creaky car and whistled his way to the crumpling hospital entrance.

The corridors were not caked with mouse droppings as Dr Clingwill walked proudly along them in his polished shoes. The elevators were not out of service, the staff rotas and health information posters were not peeling away from the walls, there was no stale odour in the air, and the stairwells were not eerily silent. As the doctor made his way up to his office carrying his bag of restricted drugs and medicines, he was back in his heyday, back in a time when everything was pristine and working. The corridors shone under his feet, the elevators pinged every two minutes as patients and visitors stepped in and out of them, the walls were gleaming with fresh paint, the air was thick with heat and disinfectant, and nurses greeted him as he ascended the stairs to the first floor.

The patients needed checking, so he didn't take too long slipping on his white coat from the hook on his office wall and dating a new report sheet. He was out in the ward in no time at all, clipboard and drugs clutched neatly in his fingers, eager to carry out his doctorly duties to the best of his ability. The six patients moaned and fidgeted on the row of beds before him, all in need of more shots and tablets. Most were men, shaggy and unshaven fifty-somethings, but at the end of the row, over to the left, lying relatively still under the sheets, was his newest patient: a teenage girl. Clingwill didn't like to indulge in favouritism as it went against his professional obligations, but someone had to be tended to first so he chose her, telling himself that she was currently more needy than the others. Her face came alive when she saw him approaching, the glazed expression lighting up a little.

'Hello Zoe,' he said, walking gracefully over to her side. He didn't need to look down at the clipboard to see her name, he'd already memorised it from the ID card in her purse. 'Let's give you some meds and vitamins. You look a little gaunt.'

As he prepared a syringe on a small steel table next to the girl's pillow, outside of her field of vision, the moans and groans from the adjacent beds rose in volume, his presence in the room causing a stir among the impaired occupants. 'They're calling out for me, bless them,' thought Clingwill, as he filled the barrel of the syringe with clear fluid. 'I'll sort them out. Nobody gets neglected on my shift.' Then, looking down towards the girl's pale face, he said, 'This won't hurt a bit.'

The girl's arm twitched and shook under his grip, her thin muscles tensing and flexing, but she was too weak to fend off the shiny tip of the needle that was sliding into her skin.

'There, all done. Calm down now, dear.

You're in no condition to start moving around just yet.'

Placing her arm back under the cover, he moved away and flitted from bed to bed, humming and whistling some old tune as he checked catheters, took temperatures, crushed tablets and recorded figures on his clipboard. Walking around the grey, dimly-lit ward, tending to the sick and needy, he was in his element, the harsh realities of the outside world all nonsense and insignificant.

Absorbed in his jobs and his duties, evening came around quickly for the doctor, and after filling out the last of his paperwork he conducted one last walk around of the ward, carrying out some final checks before clocking off for the night. With pride he concluded that his patients were in a fine condition, recovering steadily from their ailments, and after washing his hands he wished them all goodnight and turned towards the door. Over his shoulder, as he was exiting, he even heard the girl praising him, murmuring her appreciation.

'You please me, Doctor! You're the best! You're the best!'

'My pleasure, dear,' Clingwill chuckled. 'Now, do get some rest.'

With a courteous nod he closed the door, then made his way home.

'Don't leave me, Doctor! Come back! Come back!' croaked Zoe, as the doctor was preparing to leave.

She knew what this meant: the clipboard was in his hand, the rubbish had been cleared away, the sun was low and pink outside the cracked window—he was leaving for the night. What kind of doctor are you? she thought. What kind of...hospital is this? As Zoe watched him lingering by the door, trying to gauge his thoughts and intentions, his combed hair glowing in the warm sunset rays seeping in from outside, he simply smiled and told her to get some rest.

After the door clicked shut she was alone once more with the rest of the comatose patients, the sky getting darker by the minute.

ΔΔΔ

Zoe knew now that the medication, whatever it was, lost its potent edge as time went on. She'd been lying on the bed for what seemed like an eternity, listening to the gurgling and spluttering of the men in the adjacent beds, and she guessed that it must've been somewhere around 5am. The bleeps of the monitors behind her were like the incessant sounds of a broken record, a continuous playback tugging at the strings of her sanity, and she felt as though she could take no more.

Movement was coming back to her hands and feet, just as it had yesterday, and if she focused hard enough she could actually lift her head from the pillow. The grunting forms on the neighbouring beds seemed older than her, apparently lacking the energy and curiosity to question their surroundings much, but she was different, she was fighting back. Straining against the invisible hand pinning her down, the unknown concoction flowing through her veins, she tried with all her might to get her limbs moving again. She had to wrench her body out of its induced slumber, snap it back into action, and she began by pounding her heels against the springy mattress, building up a steady motion. The more she did it the easier it got, and once her legs felt alive again she moved onto her arms.

Eventually, she was able to move her hands around enough to remove her drip, and then, with a herculean effort, she pulled the bedsheet away from her and swung her legs off the edge of the mattress, dangling them a few inches above the floor. She then leapt from the edge of the bed, conducting the manoeuvre like a parachute jump, and braced herself for the landing.

The hard ground sent shockwaves through her sleepy bones, but she managed to stay upright and began walking around in her thin gown, using the moonlight from outside as a visual aid.

The plug sockets and switches in the room were in working order, she knew this because she'd observed the doctor using them, so she went straight for the light switch. The ward was suddenly illuminated in warm, yellow light, and she gazed around, dazed, taking in the various oddities surrounding her. The corners of the room were filthy with dust and grime, the bed frames rickety and old, but the equipment lying around looked functional. It was like someone had swept out an old garden shed somewhere and set it up to look like a hospital ward, imitating the real thing. The dozing patients were lined up in front of her, eyes closed, oblivious to the sudden brightness of the room. The unmistakable stench of body odour emanated from them in a huge wave, and they all seemed to have the crusty look of someone taken off the street—rather like she had, she thought, rather uneasily.

Traipsing across the room like a tranquilised gorilla, she made for the corridor outside with an aim to do some exploring. She was confused, baffled, and completely unsure of whether the hospital was genuine or not. The dirty state of the place told her it wasn't, along with the doctor's long disappearances, but...it just had to be. Why would it be anything else? It occurred to her that her drug-addicted mind might simply be playing tricks on her again, like it often did, so she was in a state of complete indecisiveness.

There was a stairwell in the corridor and she lurched towards it, holding on to the bannister for support. Her body was like a dead weight that she had to drag along, each step painfully slow and exhausting, and by the time she reached the ground floor she had to stop and sit down. Pale moonlight shone in through an array of cracks and windows, highlighting the flaky paintwork on all of the walls. The medication—as well as the drugs she'd taken the other night—still governed her bodily system, and it took everything she had to get herself back up to her feet. The sound of rats scurrying around accompanied each step, but she ignored it all and headed towards what looked like the hospital entrance.

She let herself fall into the big set of double doors and they burst open, the cold night air chilling her skin. The overgrown car park stretched out before her like a hostile wasteland, the lumpy terrain completely uninviting. The treetops she'd glimpsed from her bed were just visible in the distance, a row of black spikes pointing up towards the chalky moon. There was no way she was going to be able to make it out of the hospital grounds, not in her present state, and she fell into a heap by the open doorframe and wept at the sheer insanity of the situation. This is crazy! What am I doing? She couldn't relax in the hospital due to her dark suspicions, but at the same time she felt ridiculous crawling around the corridors in the early hours of the morning like this. What was she to do?

Out of nowhere, an idea dawned on her: phone. Shouldn't a hospital have a phone? There was obviously an electricity supply to the building, so if there was a phone somewhere it'd presumably work. And, also, it occurred to her as she slumped in the doorway, if there was a phone in the building it'd probably be on the ground floor. But who would she call? And, for that matter, what would she tell them? She hadn't the foggiest idea where she was, that was the point, so how could she lead anyone here? The answer to this conundrum, she didn't know, but she was going to try her luck and look for a phone anyway—what else was she going to do?

With a rough plan of action in mind she dragged herself back up yet again, with the speed and agility of an eighty-year-old woman, and began to search the dingy ground floor for a phone.

It took her fifteen minutes or so to find one, a wall-mounted setup with a chunky keypad, and it hung from a wall opposite a locked storage room of some kind. A faint hum came from somewhere beyond the locked wooden door, a deep vibration that she could feel under her bare feet. A generator, perhaps? It sounded like one, but she couldn't be sure, so she ignored it for the time being and focused her attention on the phone.

The earpiece was covered in dust, so it was a shock to hear a dial tone coming from it when she picked it up, but it was there. Rather tragically, there was only one person's phone number that Zoe knew completely off by heart: her main drug dealer's. This was the last number she wanted to call, but the only one that she could. But what would she say? What would she tell him?

A second idea then occurred to her: the doctor, presuming he was real, must have an office somewhere, probably close to her ward, and if she was lucky she might find something in there with his name and address on it, or maybe the address of the hospital. Putting the receiver down, she headed back to the stairs, pulling her drained body back up to the first floor.

As she'd suspected, the doctor did indeed have an office on the first floor, just beyond the ward. The stuffy little room had the feel and look of a museum exhibit, like a preserved dwelling of some long dead historical figure, everything laid out as though it'd been that way for years. This worked to her advantage, however, because after a very brief search through some of the neatly-organised drawers she found exactly what she was after: a letter with a personal name and address printed along the top of it. So you are a real doctor, Zoe muttered to herself, staring down at the words: Dr Allen Clingwill.

The horrible feeling of stupidity and humiliation ran over her again at this realisation, and she felt foolish standing there in the office dressed in just her hospital gown. The doctor was legit, and if he was legit that meant that the hospital was legit too, and if the hospital was legit that meant that she was crazier than she thought. Shit! What am I doing? I'm fucking losing it! Was it the medication playing tricks on her? Was it the alcohol, cocaine, MDMA or whatever else she'd put in her body over the last few months? Was she actually rummaging through the doctor's office in the

middle of the night, shuffling around like a confused dementia patient? She wasn't sure of anything anymore, but she knew that she had to do something, so, closing the drawers back up and leaving the office, she made her way back downstairs towards the phone.

In the silent murkiness of the downstairs corridor, leaning against the wall with the phone pressed up against her ear, she tentatively dialled the number for her main dealer, Chris, then closed her eyes and tried to compose herself. After a few rings a gruff voice echoed down the line, and she opened up to him.

'You what?' he shouted. 'What do you mean you don't know where you are?'

'Chris, please just listen to me!' she croaked. 'I can't speak for long, but I just need you to check someone out for me.'

'Check someone out?'

'Yes, the doctor. And...and maybe follow him.'

'What've you taken, Zoe? I'm in no mood to listen to you rambling on about—'

'Chris, please! I know it sounds crazy, but...I don't know, just drive over to this address and...and go from there. I need to do something! I'm desperate! I'll call you back later on this number, and you can tell me what happened.'

'But—'

'And maybe you could try to trace this phone number. Look up the area code or something.'

'What do you think I am, a fucking private detective?'

'Chris, I can't explain it! There's just something not right about this place! This is all I've got. Can you do it for me?'

'Why should I? Why should I help you out? You owe me money, for fuck's sake.'

After a moment's hesitation, Zoe said, 'I've got your money! I've got it here with me.'

'Bullshit!'

'No, Chris! I have!'

'How the fuck have you got money? You've —'

'I borrowed some a couple of days ago.'

'From who?'

'It doesn't matter, just trust me. If you do this for me, you'll get your money tonight.'

'If you're lying...If I do this and it turns out that you're lying...'

'I've got your money, Chris. I just need to find out where the hell I am.'

After another few minutes of pleading and exchanging details, she ended the call and stood quietly in the dark hospital corridor, not quite knowing what to think or feel. Gradually, out of a deep weariness, she lowered herself to a seated position under the phone and waited, hoping that Chris would do as she asked him to.

ΔΔΔ

The black sky was turning purple as Chris sped down the road in his BMW. He was tired after a night of driving around, delivering wraps and packets, but the small line he'd just sniffed was helping him to stay awake and alert. What on Earth was he doing? He had a name and address, and he was heading over there to... what? Spy on someone and follow them? It was insane. The girl owed him a lot of money, however, and that was the only thing driving him forward.

The built-in sat-nav display was declaring an ETA of three minutes, and so the tracksuit-clad, muscled young man turned the stereo off and took note of his surroundings. The street was spacious and quiet, with big trees lining the pavements and large gaps between each brick tenement. He was in a posh neighbourhood, and the sight of it immediately flicked a switch somewhere in his tearaway, petty criminal mind. Burglary was not out of bounds within his social circle, and this particular street represented an untapped goldmine.

The house he was there to look at was straight ahead on the curve of the road, and the first thing that caught his eye was the old car sitting on the driveway. It wasn't dated enough to be vintage or classic, but it wasn't new enough to be a common sight either. It kind of dampened his hopes a little bit as it wasn't exactly a display of wealth and money, but still, the big house looked as though it might've been harbouring some valuables nonetheless.

It was still dark enough to walk around without being noticed, so he parked up a decent distance away from the detached house and strolled towards it, making an effort to look as inconspicuous as possible in case anyone happened to be peering out of their windows at this early hour. Reaching the driveway, he looked down at the car with a look of pitying disgust. A pile of cassette tapes were neatly stacked in a small crevice by the gearstick, and a ripped, bent tax disc was displayed in the window that wasn't even needed anymore. What kind of twat drives a car like this? thought Chris, whose own vehicle looked luxurious and futuristic in comparison. A wide-brimmed hat and a pair of laced gloves sat on the passenger seat, clearly belonging to a woman. Some old codger and his wife, he thought, with a sardonic grin. The last thing he noticed in the car before moving on was a pile of blankets on the back seat, along with a cushion. Unsure of what to make of this, he simply shook his head and headed over towards an iron gate by the side of the house.

The gate separated the front drive from the back garden. It was locked, but he climbed over it with ease. Chris wasn't planning on breaking into the house right now, not at this hour on his own, but he did want to scope the place out a little. As soon as his feet touched the ground he could see yellow light spilling out from the rear of the house, illuminating a large patch of dewy grass across the long garden. Somebody was awake. Looking in through a side window, using the glowing light and a series of reflections, he worked out that the lit-up room was a kitchen-dining room area, with two figures sat at a table. An early breakfast, perhaps? Probably. Elderly people often got up early, and besides, the time was getting on.

With the intention of taking a quick look at the locks and windows, Chris crept along the shadows as stealthily as he could, his eyes darting around everywhere. Once he was done scoping out the side of the house he moved around the back, quickly sizing up the large back window which looked out across the garden. The locks and handles looked semi-secure, not cheap but not impenetrable either, and with a knowing smirk he swiftly turned to leave, shooting the briefest of glances through the big window towards the two occupants at the dining table as he slithered away back towards the gate.

After two paces he paused, however, frozen mid-stride.

The image of what he'd just seen through the glass flashed in his tired mind like a chilling snapshot, a surreal slide, forcing him to stop and acknowledge it. He'd clearly been awake for too long, burnt the candle at both ends for too many nights, because otherwise what he'd just seen through the window would've been real. His muscled arms tensed as he crouched there by the big dining room window, nervously bracing himself for a second viewing. He had to look again just to prove to himself that he wasn't going mad, or, conversely, to prove that he was. Positioning his head by the bottom corner of the window frame, using the leaves and branches of a potted plant for cover, he looked back in at the couple sitting at the table.

China teacups were set out in front of them, along with a pot of steaming brew. Plates of toast and jam were scattered around here and there, with an assortment of cereal boxes and cartons of milk to go with them. A lean-looking man with dark hair, presumably the one Zoe had mentioned, was chatting away to his wife in between mouthfuls of toast, his voice a muffled vibration on the other side of the glass. Rambling on, lost in the throes of conversation over breakfast, he laughed, smiled and giggled at the woman opposite him.

And it was the woman's face that'd brought Chris back to the window for a second look.

At first glance she looked extremely tanned and weathered, like she'd just got back from a holiday abroad perhaps, but upon closer inspection it became clear that her skin's imperfections ran a lot deeper than that. Her cheekbones were barely concealed by the dried-out, leathery strips that ran over them, the glow of the bulb above the table reflecting against their protruding contours. Her nose was flat and stubby, and a pair of shrivelled-up lips curled sickeningly around black gums like pieces of torn, mouldy orange peel. The eyes —or eye sockets—were little more than dusty holes in the front of a crumbling cranium, gazing across the table at the rambling man with total and utter indifference. A few wiry strands of white hair were pulled back across her peeling scalp, secured with a flowery hairband, and her dainty body sat upright with a stiff, rigid posture.

Looking in through the window at this peculiar scene, this odd, chilling scene, the young man's own body took on a similar stiffness, although his was due to terror, not decay. He was glued to the spot, unable to look away from this clothed corpse who was being spoken to by a deluded man across the table from her, drinking tea and eating mouthfuls of food. But then, just as he was starting to notice additional details from within the house: the retro-patterned wallpaper; the antique lampshade above the table; the chunky TV set in the corner, throwing grainy light from its thick screen; the silver fork that'd been carefully placed in the woman's fingers, the thin digits clasping it like rusty strands of wire; a noise rose up from somewhere out in the darkness, causing the man at the table to turn his head.

'Tanner? Is that you, boy?'

It took a few moments for Chris to register the implications of what was happening. There was a dog nearby, somewhere out in the garden with him. He could've sworn that the noise had come from somewhere else, some other garden a few rows down, but the man's reaction to it stated otherwise. He was now rising from the breakfast table, edging around the dining chairs towards the back door, and Chris turned and bolted with such explosive energy that he tripped over his own feet. He'd hardly made it two metres from the back window and he was flat on his face, elbows and knees stinging from the hard concrete.

He was still in this position when the door opened behind him, the slender figure of Clingwill leaning curiously in the frame. Chris knew he was standing there due to the silhouette cast along the ground, the new light from the doorway shining a rectangular glow across the floor with his outline in it. This new light illuminated different sections of the garden that were formerly obscured, lighting up shadows around buckets, pots, and dirty shovels that were sitting around the place. Enveloped in this bright light, Chris suddenly found himself looking into the eyes of an Alsatian dog. It'd been there all along, sitting by a wall behind him, hidden by the mauve shadows of the early morning twilight. It'd made no sound when he'd illegally entered the premises, no growls or barks, no whines or yaps, and for good reason: every crevice of its hollowed-out face was teeming with ants and bugs. Its entire head and body was as stiff and motionless as the woman's at the dining table, its dark patches of hair matted with cobwebs and bits of stone and gravel. Yellow teeth protruded from a wrinkled snout in a permanent, silent grimace, hundreds of tiny insects swarming over them like dark bloodstains.

'Tanner? What have you found?'

The man's words sent icy stabs through Chris's body, the seemingly sophisticated tone of his voice somehow adding to the horror of what was happening. Clambering up to his feet, he scarpered with more determination this time, the fear rooted within him adding spring to his step. He was back over the iron gate with the speed and agility of an Olympic hurdler, sprinting down the street towards his car without as much as a glance over his shoulder.

It wasn't until ten minutes later, flooring

his car a few miles down the road, that he realised he'd lost his wallet.

Parked up in a quiet lay-by a safe distance
away from the house, Chris lit a cigarette to
calm his nerves. What he really wanted was a
line but the wrap of powder was in his wallet, wherever the hell it was. Well, he knew
exactly where it was: it was back in that garden.
That wasn't a good thing at all, as there was a
bank card in the wallet with his name on it,
along with the packet of drugs. Could the police charge me with that? he wondered. Damn
right they could. With anybody else the answer
would've been no, but Chris had pissed the police off one too many times, so they'd definitely
find a way.

He was looking out towards the road,
puffing on his cigarette, mulling this strange
situation over in his head, when his mobile phone began to ring. The number Zoe
had called him on earlier flashed across the
screen, causing his piercing ringtone to echo
around the interior of the car. Zoe—the girl
who never paid what she owed, the girl who
always seemed to bring trouble wherever she
went, the girl who had him driving around in
the early hours of the morning even though she
was in debt to him. His wallet—an incriminat-
ing piece of evidence that could potentially get

him locked up again—was back at that house because of her. If it weren't for her sending him out on a stupid little mission, he wouldn't have lost the bloody thing. He thought about not answering it, just letting it ring and ring, but then, with a sadistic glint in his eye, a better idea occurred to him.

'Hello,' he said, pressing the green button and putting the device up against his ear.

'Chris! Chris, it's me! How...How did you get on? Did you find the address?'

Chris thought for a moment before answering, his mind on overdrive. Waves of guilt rushed through him, but his annoyance with the girl, along with her bad history, overrode it. He also had to do this; he had no option. Reporting the man to the police would inevitably lead to them finding his wallet and his drugs, and they'd never let him get away with that. There was no way he was going to go to jail for a nuisance customer like Zoe.

After taking another long drag of his cigarette, blowing smoke out of a small gap in the window, he said, as calmly as he could muster: 'Yeah, I found it.'

'And?...What—'

'It looks normal to me, Zoe. Just an old couple living in a suburban house.'

'And what about—'

'This phone number? I looked it up online, it belongs to Rachton State Hospital.'

'You mean I'm—'

'You're in the state hospital; there's nothing to worry about. Now go and get your head down and get some rest. It sounds like you need it.'

'But...are you sure? I mean, this place looks —'

'Stop panicking and get some sleep. I'll collect my money another time.'

A brief silence hung over the line, and then, after a moment, the girl's voice rose up again like a confused whisper.

'Well, if...if you're sure.'

'I'm sure,' said Chris. And then, gritting his teeth, he added, 'Goodbye Zoe,' before ending the call.

ΔΔΔ

Out in a forgotten corner of the town, the old derelict hospital sat in the dim morning light like a crumbling relic. As the sun inched its way above the horizon behind it, pink-orange rays shone in through the rotting window frames, making faint forms and objects visible within the building.

Apart from a small gathering of birds lined

up on the roof and guttering, flapping their wings and tilting their heads, and a few foxes scurrying around the empty car park, the only movement to be seen across this desolate tableau was a small figure walking along inside the ruin, traipsing past one of the illuminated window frames like a dark shadow, or ghostly apparition.

Reaching a bed, they tiredly climbed up onto it, the sun's rays outlining their movements as it crept higher up into the sky. After sitting there for a moment in a state of apparent confusion, gazing outside towards the overgrown wilderness, they slowly leant back and put their head against the pillow, ready for sleep.

FOOD FOR THOUGHT

MUSINGS ON MORTALITY

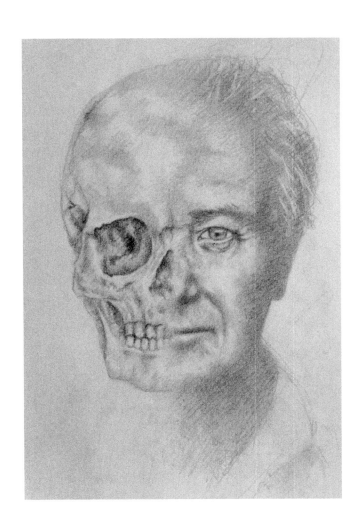

Every life is a tainted clock
Ticking into decay
The hands, they only tick downwards
Going just one way

It's always there in the background
The harsh and ugly truth
A claw that grips and catches us
For that we need no proof

With no clear way of escaping
One can only postpone
All beings, so doomed from the start
Each one is on death row

INDELIBLE STAMP

A vessel filled with luxuries, orbiting the Earth

An OAP inside it, enjoying all its worth

He wants to live forever, and has a decent plan

But the plan so rests upon, the grand advance of man

PART 1

Penfold leaned his balding head back against the edge of the large jacuzzi, letting the warm bubbles splash and burst across the wrinkled sags of his skin. Up in front of him, on the other side of the huge reinforced glass window, the curvature of planet Earth traced a wide arc across the deep blackness of space. *A giant marble sitting in a pool of black ink. That's what it looks like to me*, he mused, gazing at it dreamily from his warm, steamy tub. He'd been this way for about an hour now, lost in the view outside his spa window, literally watching the world go by as it spun its wide orbit around the sun.

His personal spa was big and spacious, the steam room, sauna and jacuzzi all kitted out with black tiles and chrome fittings. It was his favourite place on the ship by far, and he spent most of his waking hours there. The feeling of deep relaxation that he could achieve in this room was something he never tired of, never stopped yearning for, but tonight he couldn't quite get where he wanted to be.

Something was playing on his mind, his ageing brain, and it'd been nagging away at him for quite some time now. He refused to confront it, however, opting instead for a form of distraction. *A good movie, that's what I need. That'll take my mind off things.* Laying a bony hand along the rim of the big round tub, he pushed his drooping body up and out of the steamy broth, then reached for a towel.

At eighty-six years of age, Penfold had seen and done many things down on the big marble outside the window, but, even though he was approaching his ninth decade, he still wasn't through yet. The cruel afflictions of old age couldn't wear somebody down of his ilk, and he was fighting back against it with a master plan. Nature could play its nasty tricks on other people if it so wished, but it wouldn't bully Penfold.

He'd splashed out billions on his luxury ship, the ship that he'd been living on now for the last two years, and the investment had more or less wiped out his fortune, but it was all for a good reason. Earth, the big planet outside the window, had come a long way since Penfold was a child, developing technology and advanced science in abundance, but a cure for ageing was still just a thing of science fiction. The human lifespan down on that rock had lengthened considerably, but death still hadn't been conquered. And with not much more time to wait, Penfold had resorted to drastic measures. He had no family or children to worry about, anyway, no immediate heirs to his now spent fortune, so putting his cash down on this last, wild venture was worth doing as far as he was concerned.

With a towel wrapped around his bloated little potbelly Penfold shuffled along the tiled floor of his spa, his joints achy and stiff. Once he reached the end of the large room, passing his sauna and steam room, a large hatch silently slid open for him and he walked on through to his entertainment suite. The entertainment suite had a minimalist look to it, furnished with only a large screen, a long cushioned sofa, a fridge and a drinks cabinet. There was no need for anything else to be there; the sofa was easily big enough for him to stretch out on whilst watching his films, and the entertainment system built into the wall had everything stored on it digitally. When purchasing the ship, Penfold had requested just one change to the entertainment suite after the ship's manufacturers had shown it to him: a different sofa. They'd originally kitted out the suite with a hard black leather one, but he'd insisted that it was changed to a synthetic microfibre one for its higher level of comfort and durability. Leather furniture had never appealed to Penfold; it was too stiff, too sticky.

Flopping down on this microfibre sofa, he called out to the big screen on the wall, bringing it to life. 'Movies,' he said, with a trembling of his jaw. A long list of films were instantly displayed before him, a massive selection of 20th and 21st century cinema. A film lover could not have asked for anything more, he was completely spoilt for choice, but even this particular luxury still couldn't distract him from the nagging thought eating away at his mind, and he found himself unable to concentrate and choose something to watch.

After scrolling down the list for a few minutes, his thoughts somewhere else, he grumpily switched the entire system off and sat there stewing in his own torment. He knew that this time would come, he knew it all along, it was part of the grand plan after all, but still, it didn't make it any bloody easier. Penfold was a man who enjoyed his own company, and he liked being on the ship with all of its conveniences and facilities. He didn't even need to clean or dust the place, due to a special static system that he paid to have installed, so why would he want to go and plug himself into that thing out the back? *Because that's your ticket to immortality, that's why.* It was true, the pod at the back of the ship was an essential part of his plan, a key part of his strategy, but he just didn't want to do it yet. He was happy in his little life, happy having a lie in every morning then spending hours soaking in his tub, happy just... doing what he was doing. But it couldn't last forever, though, and that was the point. He only had a certain amount of years left in him, and if he wanted to get his hands on a cure for ageing, some kind of advanced technology of the future, he had to go and climb into that pod. It'd been put off for too long already, he'd spent too much time stalling and delaying the inevitable —it was time to bite the bullet and enter the next stage.

He needed to look at the thing again, that's what he needed to do. He needed to reacquaint himself with the contraption and make friends with it. It was generally something that he avoided looking at and thinking about, tucked away in the tail end of the ship behind closed doors, out of sight and out of mind. This needed to change, and now was as good a time as ever. Getting back up to his feet, dragging himself up from the sofa, he exited the entertainment suite and headed towards the back end of the vessel. He passed both his lavish bedroom and dining room on the way, resisting the urge to retreat and hide within one of them, and carried on until he got to a thick set of steel security doors marking the entrance of the rear section of the ship. The warm, relaxed atmosphere fizzled out in this part of the vessel, replaced with a feeling of cold function and austerity. This place was about purpose and practicality, business and security, and it served a hard blow after being in the stylish comfort of the spa and entertainment suite. In fact, bearing in mind that he was still wrapped in a fluffy towel, it kind of felt wrong for him to be there, but he carried on regardless.

The doors that stood before him now were unlike all the others, they didn't budge an inch as he approached, instead there was a fingerprint panel flashing and waiting for one of his digits. After a moment's hesitation he raised a veined finger and pressed it against the smooth panel, letting it scan his prints. A series of bleeping noises then rang out, followed by a click, and the heavy doors slid sideways. An automatic lighting system flickered to life as Penfold stood by the entrance of the medical suite, illuminating its various contents.

Powerful emotions swirled around his thin body as he looked across at the medical equipment, its intimidating nature causing him to sway on his feet. Right in the middle of the room, amidst a wide array of computers, digital clocks and pharmaceutical machinery, sat a large glass pod about ten feet long and three feet wide. It was a thing of great elegance and beauty, with a slick design and shiny finish, although it was hard for Penfold to appreciate it in that way.

After his nerves calmed down and subsided, he walked forward a few steps and let the thick doors close behind him.

The life pod, the most important part of the ship by far, the most valuable piece of his investment, was sitting right there before him in all its glory. The complex technology that ran through it was beyond Penfold's understanding —and beyond his caring, if the truth be told— but he understood its purpose all the same. The pod was a lottery ticket, a spin of a roulette wheel, a portal to the future.

Penfold considered it very likely that a cure for ageing would be developed on Earth eventually, some time in the not-so-distant future, but due to his age he was unable to live long enough to witness it happen and reap its benefits. Therefore he needed a way to get to the future, to live long enough to get his hands on the miracle medicine, and that's where the pod came in.

Some would call it a long shot, others would call it insane, but to Penfold it was simply an opportunity worth pursuing. Very soon he would climb into the big glass pod and lie down inside it, connecting the drips and tubes that protruded from its walls into the veins on his arms. A specially-designed cocktail of drugs would then enter his system, slow down his metabolism and heart rate, and coax his body into an induced state of hibernation. Whilst in this altered state of being his body would be able to stave off clinical death for longer than it otherwise would, giving him a chance to make it into the future. During this time science would progress back on Earth, along with medicine.

Leaving the planet to carry out this process was necessary in order to achieve the required timescale. Being in an induced state of hibernation would enable him to live for much longer, but being in a ship flying through space would enable him to live for even longer still. This particular part of the operation was also beyond Penfold's understanding, but the general gist of it was graspable. Once he was asleep inside the pod with the hibernation drugs flowing through his veins, the ship's computer would active *warp drive*, allowing the vessel to travel at insane speeds. The ship's designers had tried very hard to explain to Penfold why this was a good thing, rambling on about space and matter twisting and bending around the ship, along with something about a theory of relativity and time dilation, but the basic premise of it all was that the faster he travelled up in space, the further into the future he would be when he eventually landed back on the Blue Planet.

The pod's life support system would keep Penfold's sleeping body fed and nourished via the tubes and drips, until the sophisticated software detected that his body was in the process of winding down. When that happened, when the analysis machines detected that he only had a limited amount of time left to live, the concoction of drugs running through his system would be altered in an attempt to revive him and wake him up. In addition to this, the ship would follow a pre-programmed flight path and land back on Earth at the same location it took off from. Penfold would then reintegrate back into society, free to reap the benefits of whatever advanced technology might've emerged by that time.

All of this ran through his head as he looked down towards the shiny pod, down towards the soft bed encased within the curved glass. Fear and excitement took hold of him in equal measure, and he wondered whether it could really work. It was definitely worth a shot, certainly worth a gamble, he knew that, and after spending a few more minutes in the medical suite, checking that everything was still in working order, he decided to set a date for his hibernation.

One week seemed fitting. One more week, seven days, of lounging around in his precious ship, he thought, then it would be time for lights out.

△△△

Committing himself to this date allowed

him, paradoxically, to relax again. With a clear plan in place and a specific date set everything felt in order, and it eradicated the nagging, panicked voice within him. And with this mighty burden lifted from his shoulders, he enjoyed an immense week of hedonism. He dined on the finest selection of frozen food from his kitchen, eating mouthfuls of steak and potatoes as comets and asteroids whizzed by outside the dining room window; he sat for hours in his sauna and steam room sipping champagne, adjusting the temperature dials to his precise liking; he watched, with great enthusiasm and enjoyment, a variety of his favourite films whilst stretched out on his sofa; and each evening he lay on his big wide bed, listening to powerful symphonies and ballads on the best sound system that had ever been produced.

When the fateful day finally arrived he was slouched in his favourite place: the jacuzzi. Bubbles splashed and rippled over his liver-spotted skin as he took in the beautiful view outside the observation window one last time. The scene before him really was a wonder to behold. Distant stars and planets pierced the deep cloak of darkness with their icy white light, cutting holes through the black veil of the cosmos, twinkling away silently in the void. And then, of course, there was the round curvature of planet Earth coming in and out of view as it followed its ancient orbit, shining its blue and green hues through the thick quartz glass to reflect against the hot water of the tub. *See you in the future*, Penfold muttered, as though talking to an old friend.

Earth itself was certainly Penfold's friend, there was no doubt about that, it was humanity that he was on shaky ground with. He'd always been something of an outsider, living a semi-isolated life away from the main hordes of society. It would've been unfair to call him a misanthrope, but he was inclined at times to see the faults and errors of human behaviour. Rudeness irritated him, crime disgusted him, and several other things also used to nag away at him on a daily basis. One of which was the bizarre phenomenon of people having children when they neither had the money to feed them, nor the capability of educating them. *Breeders*, Penfold referred to them as, and they annoyed him. Why have children if you can't look after them? For something to do? For a hobby? It was just one of his pet hates; the wealthy, educated classes rarely going beyond one child, while the dregs of society tended to have at least three or four.

And then there was the traffic. Good grief, he didn't miss that at all. Tailbacks stretching from one edge of the city to the other, horns blaring for hours on end. With any luck, he thought, a new mode of transport would've been introduced by the time he got back on terrestrial soil, something cleaner and easier.

The great continents were clearly in view as Penfold gazed out, and he wondered what things looked like down there now, and indeed what they would look like in the future. Science always progressed as time went on, as did general living conditions, so despite the odd grievance he had with certain aspects of his generation, the society he'd be joining when he woke from his long slumber would surely be a good one. A new era awaited him, and tears welled up in his eyes as he watched his home planet spin away. It was an emotional moment knowing that he'd never see it the same way again, knowing that the place, the people, the ethos, and the technology would all be altered in some way when he relanded. *It's time. I'll go crazy if I sit here any longer.* Struggling to control this unexpected weeping, he pulled his naked form up and out of the steamy water for the last time, ready to start his long sleep.

He would've been at a loss to describe what he was feeling as the doors to the medical suite slid open, revealing the waiting glass capsule. Fear? Anxiousness? No, he was past all of that, but still, something fluttered around inside of him. The life pod looked different now, more real perhaps, like it was cast in a different light. Up until now it'd been a display prop or a museum exhibit, sitting there like an unused showpiece, but now it looked like a real piece of medical equipment ready to eat him up.

He was required to enter the pod naked, which was fine since he only had his jacuzzi towel wrapped around him once again. He slowly untied it from around his waist and stashed it away in one of the many small compartments that lined the room, suddenly wondering what it would look like and smell like when he re-emerged from the pod eons down the line. The ship's engineers and designers had thought of everything, programming the vessel to land on complete autopilot when his body grew weaker, as well as installing drainage systems and what not for the spa room, but what would become of his sweaty towel? *Only time will tell*, he thought, and then turned his attention back to the bigger task at hand.

Standing naked before the transparent, sterile capsule, he felt like an aged baby ready to crawl back into an artificial, electronic womb. And this was true, in a sense. Its sealed casing would indeed enclose him and enshroud him like a warm maternal stomach, and its wires and tubing would feed him and nourish him like an array of umbilical cords. He stepped closer to it, gingerly, tentatively, then pressed a button on its digital control panel. The glass casing rolled open sideways with a smooth, mellow hum, inviting him into its clinical embrace with open arms. Taking extra care not to lean on any other buttons or switches, he awkwardly climbed into the thing and then made himself comfortable on the bedding. There was another set of buttons and switches available to him inside the pod, right next to his head, and he pressed the relevant one to close the lid again, watching as the curved glass went over him like a frozen wave.

Several times during the last week, in between watching his favourite films, Penfold had played the instructional videos installed on his entertainment system by the ship's designers, so he was fairly confident that he knew what to do. All of the medication was measured and prepared already, waiting to swim around his blood stream, so all he really had to do was administer it. It was straight forward enough, but still, he wasn't really looking forward to jabbing himself with needles. He had a squeamish side to him, there was no doubt about that, so securing the drips in place would require a little bit of bravery and determination.

There were three of them in total, each one protruding from the inner walls of the pod like a white serpent ready to bite. Each one had its own specific job. One of them would feed him the cocktail of drugs that would put him to sleep and slow his body down, one would supply him with a steady flow of vitamins and nutrients, and the other one would keep him hydrated with water. This hydrating tube would, of course, require him to insert a catheter into his penis to prevent his urine from spilling out over the bed. Unfortunately, this had to be done first, so, ignoring the three main drips for the time being, he set about putting this urinary catheter in place. And it was, quite possibly, the most uncomfortable thing Penfold had ever done. It went against all of his instincts to insert the hard plastic tubing into the end of his withered member, watching it disappear further and further into his shrivelled shaft, but he gritted his teeth and persevered like a trooper, pushing it until it was firmly lodged in place.

It was a relief to have the catheter in place, but now he had to deal with the drips. According to the instructional videos he was to connect the hydrating tube first, so he picked up one of the available syringes and peeled off its protective plastic wrapping. The tip of the needle was razor sharp with a section of plastic tubing surrounding it, and he guided it towards the bulkiest vein that he could see on the inside of his forearm. It rested against his saggy, wrinkled skin, eager to pierce it, but Penfold couldn't sink it in straight away, he had to psyche himself up a little bit. It took a few moments for him to get himself in the right frame of mind, and when he was there he pushed delicately but firmly. The needle sank into him with a cold, icy stab, then he pulled it back out, leaving just the plastic tubing in place. After putting the used syringe in a small compartment by his side, he connected the drip to the hydrating tube and the job was done. It was unpleasant, but not terrible. And now that the first one was out of the way, it allowed him to move onto the others with more speed and efficiency.

The vitamin drip was next, and he inserted it into another prominent vein, this time on his opposite arm. He now had a drip sticking out of each one of his arms, restricting his movement somewhat, but it was imperative to get the third one in as well. The third one was the big one, figuratively speaking that is, and Penfold was well aware that once it was in he'd only have a few minutes of consciousness left before nodding off into a deep, deep slumber. *This is it. This is really it.* The moment Penfold had planned, prepared, sweated over, worried about, and obsessed over for so long was finally upon him, and it felt surreal. He was about to enter the next stage of his life, a new era, and he couldn't quite believe it was happening. His brain was a ball of fuzz, his thoughts a jumble of static, but he had to keep things together for just another minute or so. *Come on, pull yourself together and do this.* He unwrapped the third needle and guided it over towards his left arm —the arm closest to his heart. After a deep breath he inserted the plastic tubing using the needle, placed the needle in the small compartment, connected the last drip, then leaned back down against the bedding.

According to the information that he'd been given he now had just a few minutes before the drugs kicked in, sending him off into a state of deep oblivion. Using the small control panel by his head, he activated the pod's AI system then stared through the glass casing towards the ceiling. The white lights of the medical suite shone down at him, piercing and bright, but gradually, as the seconds wore on, they grew dimmer and dimmer, losing their intensity, until eventually they fizzled out altogether, along with Penfold's awareness and conscious state of being.

PART 2

*S*omething was wrong, Penfold thought. He'd closed his eyes for a brief second, and now they were open again. The bright lights of the medical suite shone down at him through the lid of the glass pod, burning away. *Had the drugs not worked?* They must've done something to him because he felt drowsy, but they were supposed to do a lot more than make him feel drowsy. In an effort to detect the problem he went to lean up from the pillow to inspect the drips in his arms, but found that he couldn't; not straight away, anyway. His body felt as though it'd been trampled upon by an elephant, or maybe a herd of them, and it took a good deal of stretching and writhing until he could move around semi- comfortably. All of the drips were in place, and no error alerts were sounding off from anywhere on the pod's computer, so, realising this, Penfold began to wonder whether he'd actually just woken up from his hibernation.

After pressing a button on the interior control panel, he painfully sat up and looked over towards one of the digital clocks on the far wall. The date and time displayed on the clock looked so strange and unfamiliar, his first

258

thought was that it must've been incorrect. But there was no reason to doubt it, and so his creased face lit up with excitement. If he'd been able to, if it weren't for the fact that his throat felt like a strip of sandpaper, he would've cried out in amazement and disbelief. He'd made it to the future, he'd done it. An unbelievable amount of time had just passed by in the blink of an eye, and now he was back on Earth. Penfold thought about this last part for a second, though. *Am I back on Earth?*

There were no windows in the medical suite, so for all he knew he could still be flying through deep space. He needed to investigate and have a look around, but the very prospect of climbing out of the pod seemed as daunting as climbing Mount Everest. He dared not remove any of the drips yet, either, in case his body went even weaker from the sudden lack of vitamins and water. The only thing he could really do for now, he decided, was remain in the pod until his hibernation fatigue had worn off a bit.

And then, and only then, could he find out for sure if he really was back on planet Earth.

△△△

As Penfold walked through the ship's innards, his bones and joints felt as stiff as rusty hinges. Each step was a slow, creaky one, but at least he was back on his feet again. It'd taken a while for him to climb out of the pod, his disorientation preventing him as much as his stiff body, but he now felt as though he had his wits about him again.

It was an odd experience to see all of his belongings again. Everything, of course, was exactly where he'd left it, and seeing it all sitting there with the knowledge of how much time had passed filled him with a strange emotion that he couldn't identify.

He traipsed around his bedroom for a while, putting on some loose clothing, building up the courage to walk through to the spa. The spa's observation window would provide him with a clear view of whatever was outside, and he was nervous about seeing it. This would be a huge moment for him, his first glimpse at the future, and, like everything else involved in this venture, it required a little bit of preparation.

In he went, through the sliding doors of the spa, walking carefully across the black tiles. Barely halfway across the room he stopped, however, stunned and dumbfounded, staring out towards the unfamiliar scene. The black carpet of space was no longer there on the other side of the window; the swirling cosmos, with all of its comets and twinkling stars, had been replaced with a concrete landscape.

For a long while he could do nothing but stand there and gape at the picture before him, marvelling at the sight of solid ground and blue sky. The ship appeared to be sitting on a large runway, and that made sense since it'd been programmed to land back down at Evergress City Airport where it'd taken off all those years ago. The ship—or perhaps, the engineers—had apparently done its job properly, and Penfold now accepted that he was back in his home city. This fact should've made him elated, jumping for joy, but he wasn't celebrating because something wasn't quite right. Everything seemed too quiet and desolate outside, with no kind of activity going on whatsoever. His arrival at the airport had apparently gone completely unnoticed, and that was odd because Evergress City Airport was, or at least had been, a hub of constant flights and bustle. Nobody had come to greet him, there were no pilots or runway workers about, nor were there any planes taking off or refuelling. The entire area looked dead, vacant and unused.

Before Penfold could even think about leaving the ship, he had to get some food inside him. There was still plenty of food on board for him, and he prepared himself a ready meal with minimal effort. After eating he felt a little bit stronger, and ready to face the outside world. His spirits had dampened slightly after seeing how empty everything was outside, but he needed to explore before jumping to any conclusions.

The ship's airlock and exit doors were tightly sealed, but they opened with the tap of a button. This was quite a momentous event in itself because, for the first time in years, fresh, natural, terrestrial air filled Penfold's nostrils and mouth. It was a shock, and it felt moist and warm on his tender throat, bringing back hazy memories of a time gone by. A stairway had extended down from the ship, all the way down to the ground, and he descended it. The sight of an open sky above his head damn near took his breath away, and he stared up at the fluffy clouds like a child seeing them for the first time.

Once his shock and disorientation had subsided, he turned his attention back towards the airport itself and his immediate surroundings. There were around a dozen or so planes scattered across the runway, all stationary and inert. They were of a kind Penfold had never seen before, edgy and futuristic in their shape and design, but each and every one of them was covered with a thick layer of mould and grime. It was obvious that the planes had been inactive for some time, and the wild tufts of long grass that were sprouting up from the ground here and there were extra proof of this.

He approached the plane closest to him, a

large passenger jet with huge wings spread out on either side of it. Its aerodynamic body had been designed to perfection, surpassing anything from Penfold's era, but the whole thing was riddled with cracks and rust. He stood staring up at the huge machine, feeling like an ant gazing up towards a giant bird, dismayed somewhat at its tragic decay. The tips of its wings were hanging loose, its tires were flat, and its once-white paintwork had turned to a sickly mix of green and beige. The contrast of advanced, futuristic design and ancient, mouldy decay messed with Penfold's head. This plane clearly belonged to the future, it even made his own spaceship look outdated and old fashioned, yet it was sitting there like some kind of forgotten antique.

The windows of the massive jet were too high up and too obscured with grime to see into. There were several of them running along the side of it in a neat row, all round and compact, but they revealed no clue as to what was inside the huge vessel. A set of mobile steps, rather like the one on his ship, was positioned against the body of the plane and Penfold contemplated climbing up them to see if he could gain access. But, just as he was assessing the safety of doing so, a mighty crash erupted from somewhere inside the plane. His heart instantly pounded against the walls of his chest as he realised someone, or something, could be inside the massive jet after all, and he shakily edged away from it.

What was *that?* Penfold thought. *Did an object inside the plane fall over on its own? Did a piece of panelling fall out of place due to age and decay, or was there somebody in there?* These thoughts were dizzying him and driving him crazy as he looked up towards the monstrosity of glass and steel, and then, seemingly out of nowhere, a hand pounded the inside of one of the small round windows. He saw it happen, a large palm slapping against the filthy glass, accompanied by a throaty scream. That was enough; he turned and ran as fast as his twig-like legs could carry him, his stiff body straining under the extra exertion. This banging and screaming continued behind him as he hobbled along the grassy runway, and it turned his grey hairs up on end with fright.

As soon as he was a safe distance away he slowed down a little, drawing huge lungfuls of air into his tired body. This was not a good start, not what he'd been hoping for, and the rising dread that was already present in his gut rose some more and grew in intensity. The main airport terminal was up in front of him, looking just as dilapidated and ruined as the planes, and his mind filled with dark thoughts as he studied its outline against the sky. *What the hell is going on? Has the airport been taken over by squatters or criminals? Have I just accidentally landed in mob territory?*

Penfold was actually familiar with the general layout of the airport, having been there several times during his former life, and so he knew that the exit to the grounds was behind the big main terminal up ahead. Picking up his pace once more, scurrying along, shuffling his sagging body across the vast tarmac and concrete, he headed for the exit gates on the other side of the crumbling terminal building. Frantic, agitated noises rose up all around him as he did so, however, echoing across the vast airport grounds. Muffled cries rang out from various nearby planes, shouts of mania and insanity, and blurred figures could be seen running and dancing around inside the airport terminal itself. Pockets of people were present in the old building, that he was sure of, groups of unruly beings jumping and yelling at him from behind the fogged glass panelling, more hands pounding away at walls and windows. *Who are these people? What do they want?* Penfold was in a world of shit, a whirlwind of mystery and uncertainty, and he had to get away from the airport if he was to have any chance of thinking clearly.

Outside the airport, on the other side of the rusty chain-link fence that enclosed it, Penfold fell to his knees in exhaustion. The

shadowy outline of the airport terminal building sat there in the distance, flanked by the
assortment of crumbling planes, and it was a
very depressing sight that drained away his optimism. Something had occurred here, some
kind of massive societal breakdown, and he
dearly hoped that it was confined to just this
one area. Other parts of the city were visible to
the east of his position in the form of rooftops,
but his eyesight wasn't sharp enough to make
out many details. *Are those office blocks clean
and functional, or are they abandoned and crumbling like everything in this airport?* Penfold wondered, as he squinted over towards the jagged
cityscape a few miles out. There was only one
way for him to find out, of course, and so once
he'd recovered from his trauma he climbed
back up to his feet and made his way east.

△△△

It took a while to get into the city, and
Penfold's feet were aching from the long walk.
Sat on an old bench by the side of the road,
he rested and took in the surroundings. To his
dread and disappointment, the entire street
that he was on looked just as bad as the airport.
The road was being taken over by thick clumps
of weeds and grass, and all of the buildings
were derelict. One particular building caught

his eye, a tall office block directly opposite him on the other side of the road. It rose up towards the sky like a giant rotten tooth, its brickwork dark with moss and its window frames hollow and empty. Various pieces of debris were scattered across the building's entrance, bent chairs, smashed computer monitors, broken filing cabinets, etc, and it looked to Penfold like the place had been looted for all its contents.

There was hardly a sound to be heard from anywhere, but then, out of nowhere, a series of piercing screams rang out from the old office block, not unlike the ones he'd heard earlier at the airport. With a cacophony of scrapes, bangs and angry cries, a handful of people then came tumbling out of the building's entrance, as naked as the day they were born. They were punching and kicking each other in a wild frenzy, going for each others' throats, and Penfold's first instinct upon seeing this display of lunacy was to get up and run to safety. He didn't end up running, though, because they were all so involved in their scrap that they were oblivious to his presence across the road. Instead he hunched his shoulders slightly, making himself as inconspicuous and quiet as possible, and discreetly watched the bizarre spectacle with absolute astonishment. He couldn't believe what he was seeing, he couldn't fully accept it, not because the people were naked and fighting in the street, but because the people weren't actually people at all—they were chimpanzees.

At least, that's what they looked like at first glance. After watching them for a little while longer, jumping and yelling and clawing at each other, it became apparent that they were different from any chimpanzee that Penfold had ever seen in the past. Although they shared the same basic anatomy as standard chimpanzees, with big round earlobes and long arms and legs, they carried themselves differently and had numerous features that didn't match. The animals that he was looking at, whatever they were, stood taller with a bipedal gait and had more dexterity about them. There was only one thing that Penfold could think of that could possibly explain this. These creatures must've been descendants of chimpanzees of the past, escapees from a zoo or enclosure somewhere perhaps, who'd progressed onto another stage of evolution. An enormous amount of time had passed since he'd left Earth, not very long in evolutionary terms, but long enough for change to have occurred nonetheless, so this was a plausible explanation. How they'd come to occupy the city, though, he had no idea.

They were using their hands deftly and skilfully, picking up discarded office equipment to hit each other with. From the seclusion of the bench, he watched as broken keyboards were picked up and swung like cricket bats, computer monitors were hurled across the air like boulders, and bent swivel chairs were smashed across heads. Witnessing this ferocity and boisterousness, Penfold speculated that these creatures may have driven out the residents of Evergress City purely by their domineering presence. It was only speculation, though, and he didn't have a definite answer. Maybe the citizens of the city had left of their own accord, due to some random freak event or circumstance, then the animals simply filled the gaps that were left over in their absence.

The scuffle ended after five minutes or so, and the primate creatures grumpily wandered off in various directions, alternating between bipedalism and quadrupedalism depending on the terrain. What was he to make of all this? What was he to do? Evergress City had been taken over by animals, and he was stranded there alone. Could there still be a human population somewhere? A community that he could be a part of? More exploring was in order, he decided, more hunting for civilisation. When he was ready he took off again, hobbling past the deserted shops and dented car shells like a lost soul.

△△△

A dark suspicion began to form in Penfold's

mind the more he studied these creatures. He was stood next to an old petrol garage, dusty and unused just like everything else, with a row of adjacent pylons stretching off behind it into the distance. The sky was still clear and bright with the sun giving off an intense glow, and dark blots were visible halfway up some of the steel pylon structures as members of this primate breed dangled and curled themselves around them as though they were climbing frames. This crass, chimpanzee-like behaviour reassured him slightly, pushing the dark suspicion away and making it less likely, but the Homo sapien-like behaviour scared him. The most blatant of which happened right there by the petrol station forecourt.

Hurried footsteps rose up behind him as he stood there by the cracked fuel pumps, causing him to turn his head. As he did so a stray dog came rushing past him, running for its life, followed by a pack of six foot-tall primates in hot pursuit. The pack, a group of four, were all armed with makeshift spears made from steel fence posts, jogging along and taking aim at the terrified hound. For a split second, as Penfold watched the group run along barefoot with their spears held high, he felt as though he was witnessing a scene from the ancient African savannah. It was a picture straight out of a textbook on human evolution, the early days of mankind, and its implications were enormous.

Were these modern day chimpanzees taking the same evolutionary path as humans did millions of years ago? Had they begun their long journey towards abstract thought and civilisation? Or, as Penfold was beginning to wonder, was something else at play here?

Their naked, fuzzy bodies shot past him with a chorus of grunts and huffs, almost knocking him over. They completely ignored him during their big chase, their primitive hunt for supper, but it was an intimidating experience all the same. And what an additional blow to Penfold's optimism this was, what a dimming of his hopes to find some anti-ageing technology. His mission objective was becoming a joke, a dream that was unlikely to ever happen, and if this dark theory of his turned out to be true it would definitely never happen. He was now desperate to find some human beings, desperate to find some people who could both help him cure his old age and simultaneously prove to him that humanity hadn't...well, the idea was too grim to even contemplate, so he pushed it away and buried it.

Fatigue and hunger were beginning to wear him down. He'd been walking for quite some time now, and if he didn't find food or people soon he would be in serious trouble. Further down the main road that he was on, beyond the metal pylons with the furry bodies hanging from them, warehouses and skyscrapers rose up from the horizon. If he was going to find anything it would be there, he acknowledged to himself, before continuing along on his one-man-trek through the carcass of the city.

△△△

Following these buildings on the horizon, Penfold ended up in Central Evergress City—or the remains of it, at least. A once-thriving part of the city, the whole area had a wide array of surviving architecture, and the primate population seemed to grow in density, too. He was in a bad way, his frail body shaky and jittery from a lack of nutrients, and he'd reached a stage now where he was preparing himself for the worst. He was basically drifting along, seeing how far he could go, not really expecting to find anything other than more lowly beasts and crumbling concrete. A surprising amount of stray dogs and foxes were scurrying around the alleyways and small lanes, tempting him with the idea of catching one for food, but he lacked the energy and speed to even do that.

A flimsy-looking warehouse building caught his attention not far from where he stood, mainly due to some faint noises that were ringing out from it, and he hobbled over towards it. A warehouse seemed like a likely place to find some food and, sure enough, as he reached the open shutters he could see another pack of chimps scrabbling around a discovered cache of ancient stock. He was able to enter the premises undetected due to the preoccupation of the primates—not that he really cared anymore whether they saw him or not—and he sat himself down by a stack of flaking pallets and warped iron shelving.

The discovered booty was a few tins of beans that'd been dug up from a hole in a sunken patch of floor, and the chimps were going crazy for it. Penfold would've eaten some too, but there wasn't enough left worth fighting for. He watched as they smashed the tins against the floor repeatedly until the cold contents spilled out, then slurped the juice with their tongues. Some of the more sophisticated ones had the gumption to use shards of broken shelving to cut into them instead, however, thus reducing waste. They were using tools again, Penfold noted, a rudimentary form of tin opener, prising the tins open with controlled wrist movements.

He knew the truth before the definitive evidence came. Sitting there in the corner, slumped against the wall feeling his life draining away, he knew exactly what these creatures were who pottered around in front of him. Proof was unnecessary, it was too obvious, but nevertheless, as he watched this primitive feeding frenzy he got some undeniable proof that his theory was correct. Amidst the ripping and cutting of tins, and the howling of hunger, a series of sounds came out of the creatures that very closely resembled English.

'Mmm...minnnne.'

'Ggg...ggiivvee. Gggiivvee mmeee!

It came from an agitated pair who were fighting over one of the last archaic tins, pulling it back and forth between them whilst shouting in each others' faces. These brutes weren't the descendants of chimpanzees at all, they were the descendants of humans; or, more specifically, they were the descendants of the residents of Evergress City. There was no doubt in Penfold's mind about this, he knew it was the truth. While it would've been possible for a different species to develop speech and language, there's no way that a different species would accidentally develop English. It went against all odds, it just wouldn't happen. The citizens of Penfold's era had evolved, but instead of progressing and building upon their past achievements they'd regressed back to something anachronistic. Now they were lost, completely incapable of understanding or working the technology around them.

Slouching against the rotting pallets, staring across the warehouse floor like a dying patient on a hospital bed, Penfold was reminded of his observations and hang ups about the city's former society. He remembered the way that the poor and uneducated bred with a passion, their desire to have large families unstoppable and unfaltering, whilst the wealthy bourgeois rarely went beyond one child. An unhealthy trend had been present in the old days, a backwards way of thinking, where people had children out of a lack of ambition and aspiration, and that cruel hobby had ultimately resulted in this blatant reduction in progress and IQ.

As these dim-witted hominids wrestled each other for scraps of food, muttering broken English through their blackened teeth, Penfold wondered about the scale of this reversion. Was it confined to Evergress City, or had the entire world taken a backwards step? The connection between poverty and overbreeding had certainly been a worldwide phenomenon back in the day, with the poorest countries producing the biggest families, so had the same thing happened across all countries and continents?

This was a question that Penfold would never know the answer to, because he found himself unable to rise back up from his makeshift seat. He was now collapsed across the splinters of wood, his eyes glazed and his mouth drooling and gaping, his energy reserves well and truly spent. *So be it*, he whispered, sensing his impending demise. This horrific discovery had extinguished his yearning for immortality, making death seem almost pleasant by comparison. The miles of decaying streets he'd seen since landing back down on Earth now represented the failure of humanity, every moss-covered shopfront a symbol of regression, every pile of dust and rubble an emblem of the collapse of progress. The futuristic city he'd hoped for didn't exist, instead he'd landed down upon a re-enactment of the savage days of pre-civilisation, a backwards world where lower life forms puzzled over the inventions of a time gone by.

This was it, his last, final resting place, a dusty corner of an unused storage building, and the last thing he saw before drifting off into his longest of long sleeps, was the wild thrusts of passion as the beasts before him indulged in some post-meal fornication and procreation, giving in to their carnal desires and adding to their numbers.

We must, however, acknowledge, as it seems to me, that Man with all his noble qualities, with sympathy which feels for the most debased, with benevolence which extends not only to other men but to the humblest living creature, with his god-like intellect which has penetrated into the movements and constitution of the solar system—with all these exalted powers—Man still bears in his bodily frame the indelible stamp of his lowly origin.

Charles Darwin

THE DEVOTED DROID

The ship was a thing of beauty, sailing through the void

And roaming around inside, there was a servile droid

The crew seemed elusive, they were nowhere to be seen

But even in their absence, the droid was nice and keen

PART 1

Neville stared silently out of the cockpit window, watching the stars and gas clouds glide by in the distance. His partner, Shane, was sat next to him, also silent and pensive. Neville was piloting the Sprintjet in which they both sat, working the controls with impressive dexterity. Being a tiny, aerodynamic vessel designed for high speed and maneuverability, the Sprintjet cut through the vacuum of space like a small bird flying across a windless field.

Usually, towards the end of a mission, Neville would be relaxed, leaning back in the cockpit seat in a calm, collective manner, but right now he felt edgy and nervous. His podgy face was etched with worry, and his blue eyes were tainted with fear. The two of them were on their way back from a scouting mission, checking out new moons and planets for possible mining locations, but they'd found zilch. Their strict superiors back on Erilon would be furious about this, and they knew it.

Erilon, the merciless, ruthless empire, is situated on Mars. Its citizens are direct descendants of the first—and only—Mars colonists from Earth, although people on Earth nowadays rarely acknowledge its existence out of shame and embarrassment. Cutting its ties with Earth authorities and becoming self-sufficient and independent, the Erilonian Empire soon transformed into a dictatorial regime. Failure in any kind of task was frowned upon by those in charge, and returning from something as important as a scouting mission with no results, no new mining coordinates, was a punishable offence. With this in mind, it was understandable that both Neville and Shane were nervous about returning back to base. And as if this wasn't disastrous enough, things were about to get a whole lot worse.

'Shit,' muttered Neville, looking down at an ominous cluster of green dots advancing steadily across the screen of the Sprintjet's control panel.

'What is it?' asked Shane, leaning his wiry body over to have a look.

'It looks like a meteor shower. And it's coming our way.'

'How big is it, exactly?'

'At least twenty miles wide,' said Neville, wiping sweat from his brow.

'Well, just fly around it then. Plot a new course.'

'Yeah...' mumbled Neville, his voice trailing off.

'What is it? What's the problem?'

'It's...It's going to be a big diversion. I just

hope that we don't—'

'No! Don't say it! Don't tell me you forgot to load up on emergency fuel again!'

'Look, don't worry, I think we'll make it. I just—'

'You *think* we'll make it? Oh, this just gets better and better, doesn't it? We're already in the shit for coming back with nothing, and now it turns out that you're in neglect of your duties! I don't believe it!'

'Calm down, will you? We should make it. As long as this shower isn't too big.'

'Well let's hope it's not,' snapped Shane, his chiselled features screwing up in disgust. Then, under his breath, he added, 'For your bloody sake.

△△△

A colossal assortment of rocks and boulders hurtled through the void of space, shooting across the inky blackness like medieval cannon fire. The range and variety was immense; some were a mere two inches wide, others the size of football stadiums. Now that they were safely out of the way of this bombardment of cosmic stones Neville and Shane breathed a sigh of relief, but they both knew that their worries were still far from over. The meteor shower had forced them to take a one hundred and twenty-three mile detour, much larger than expected, and fuel was running low. They were now flying through uncharted territory miles away from Mars, but Neville was hesitant to send out a distress call to base because he knew what kind of punishment would await him if he did. He was clinging on to the dim hope that he might make it back to Erilon without assistance, flying the Sprintjet along at a slow, steady, fuel-saving speed.

'We're never going to make it back,' said Shane. 'We're too far out. You're going to have to put out a distress call.'

'I'm not putting out a distress call. If we cruise along at a steady speed, we should make it.'

'We *should* make it? You keep saying...' Shane stopped mid-rant, distracted by Neville's gaze towards the monitor. 'What's the matter? What is it now?'

'I don't know. There's something else showing up.'

'Well it's not a meteorite,' said Shane, looking over at the new green dot on the screen. 'It looks more like a...'

'Like a ship,' said Neville, his voice laced with trepidation.

'Zoom in on it, will you? Let's get a closer look at it.'

Neville zoomed in and an enlarged image of the mystery vessel appeared on the screen in front of them. It was unlike anything either of them had ever seen before. The central body of the ship was shaped like a massive round hockey puck, with five long columns protruding from it to form a star shape. As this strange craft headed their way it resembled a huge spinning snowflake or propeller, its long arms and columns painted with a striking shade of white.

'I'm sending a communication request,' said Neville, tapping some buttons on the controls.

'You're what?'

'You heard me.'

'Well...Is that really wise?! We've got no idea who it is.'

'They might be able to refuel us,' said Neville, frantically typing out a message.

Shane began to protest but then stopped himself, knowing full well that if they could manage to get refuelled it'd be of huge benefit to them.

'It looks like it could be a research vessel,' said Neville, once the request had been sent.

'You think so?'

'Yes. Maybe a private one from Earth.'

'Is it really likely that they're going to help us if they're from Earth?'

'Possibly, yes,' said Neville, after some consideration. 'The big civilisations on Earth are known for their liberal tendencies.'

'I'm really not sure about this, Neville.'

'We've got a reply!'

'What does it say?' said Shane, closing his eyes.

'It's a set of docking instructions. I think they're inviting us aboard!'

As they both sat stiffly in the Sprint-jet's cockpit, staring out the window like two scared lambs, the daunting outline of the spindly vessel appeared before them, crawling through the black mist of space like a giant white spider.

Neville headed towards a landing port that'd opened up on the side of the big ship, flying with care and attention. With a considerable amount of skill and concentration, he entered through the hatch and landed in the designated chamber. Within seconds of their entry the hatch closed behind them, sealing them in an airlock.

The pair of them disembarked and cautiously eyed up their surroundings. Dim orange overhead lighting allowed them to see the outlines of metal grates and girders all around them, and an array of steel pipes snaked along every corner of the large room. Once they could see that there was no immediate danger, they began to walk around. Their footsteps echoed around the metallic architecture, and the air was cold and stale. Both of them had their concerns, but before either of them could say anything to each other, a tall door slid open at the top of a long staircase in front of them, leaving a bright rectangular opening that shone piercing light down into the landing port. This sudden illumination was dazzling and disorientating, but the blinding light was eased when a dark silhouette appeared in the open door frame, watching them silently.

Neville's brain was in "fight or flight mode" as he stood at the bottom of the stairs, and he could also hear Shane shuffling around behind him as though he too was preparing to take some kind of action. *Who was this man looking down at them? Had they just walked into a trap?* Just as he thought he was about to explode under the sheer intensity of the situation, the man up in the doorway started to speak.

'Greetings. My name is Zentalver. Welcome aboard The *Wanis* Research Vessel. Do you require any assistance?'

The man's tone was extremely courteous and formal, and it had an instant calming effect on both of them, putting them at ease.

'Go on,' whispered Shane, 'it was your idea to come here. Answer him.'

'Erm, yes,' said Neville, clearing his throat. 'We come from Mars, and our ship is low on fuel.'

After a lengthy pause the figure in the doorway said, 'Well, you've come to the right place, my friends. I think I may be able to help you, but first let me prepare you some refreshments. Please, let me take you up to the recreation suite.'

They both looked at each other, trying to gauge each others' thoughts. Zentalver seemed friendly enough, but they could hardly even see him up there in the bright doorway, so they had no idea who they were really dealing with. On the other hand, they were in a very sticky situation and it'd be silly to turn away an offer of help.

'Shall we?' said Neville.

Shane nodded, grudgingly, and they both began to climb the metal stairs.

Up close, Zentalver had a handsome appearance. He wore a thin beige spacesuit with dark boots, and had a firm build. His skin looked clean and smooth, and a wave of black hair swept over his round scalp. There was an awkward feeling as they travelled up in the ship's elevator, though, due to his apparent lack of small talk and social skills, but it was soon realised that he was some kind of service droid. When Zentalver spoke he did so with impeccable manners and precision, but he only spoke if the situation required him to do so. Although he didn't seem to be a threat, it came as a relief when the lift doors opened to the recreation suite.

'Please make yourself at home while I prepare you some refreshments,' said Zentalver, walking out into a bright kitchen area.

They sat themselves down on some cushioned chairs while Zentalver walked off to prepare beverages. The recreation suite was comfortable, spacious, and very clean. A pool table was in the centre of the room, and a row of entertainment systems lined the far wall. Everything was very luxurious and pristine, with plenty of facilities, but at the same time it seemed to have an empty, unused feel to it. Apart from the deep hum of the ship and the clattering noises coming from Zentalver's direction, there were no sounds to be heard.

'Feels a little bit creepy to me,' said Shane, looking around. 'I haven't seen anyone else here apart from the droid.'

'Well, let's not jump to any conclusions. Hopefully we won't be here long, so let's just relax and let him refuel the Sprintjet.'

'Relax? How can I relax knowing that we're in—'

'Here are your drinks, gentlemen.'

Zentalver appeared out of nowhere, holding two glasses full of ice water. Neville leaned forward to retrieve his drink.

'Thank you, Zentalver.'

Shane snatched his glass, then, rather abruptly, said, 'So you're a droid, then?'

Neville almost choked on his water as he heard this, appalled at his partner's bluntness.

The two of them had very different opinions when it came to droids and robots, but thankfully Zentalver didn't seem to take any kind of offence.

'How kind of you to notice. Yes, I am a maintenance droid. I was designed and built specifically to repair and maintain the *Wanis* Research Vessel.'

Listening to his traditional English tone, Neville wondered who'd programmed him, and who's voice he'd adopted. He refrained himself from asking this question, however, choosing not to stoop down to Shane's insensitive level. He asked another question instead, a more important question, a question that both he and his partner wanted to know the answer to.

'So, Zentalver, where's the...where's the, err...the rest of the crew?'

There was a slight pause as Zentalver processed the question, the expression on his face remaining still and unchanged.

'The crew are due to return any time now.'

'They're not onboard?'

'Not at the moment, but they will be. They had to evacuate due to a technical fault that we experienced, but I've fixed the problem now and have informed them of the update.'

'They had to evacuate because of a technical fault?' said Shane, dubiously.

'Yes. There was a problem with some of the wiring in the central hub, and it constituted a fire hazard. The safety of the crew is imperative; it was essential that they evacuated.'

'How big is the crew?' Neville asked.

'The crew consists of thirty individuals, all scientists and apprentices.'

'But where exactly are they? Where did they evacuate to?'

'They are orbiting the ship in six separate lifepods.'

'We didn't see them on our radar,' said Shane, giving Neville a side glance.

'They are following a wide orbit for safety reasons. Their safety is imperative.'

'Are you all from earth?' asked Neville.

'*Wanis* is a terrestrial vessel, yes.'

Shane scowled as he heard this. Like most Erilonians he'd been brought up to be very wary of Earthlings, and he generally held them in contempt. He'd already concluded that the ship must've been from Earth, but hearing this confirmation still caused a wave of disgust to ripple up inside of him. He wanted to get off this weird, creepy ship as soon as possible. 'How long will it take you to refuel our Sprint-jet?' he asked, rather bluntly.

'A couple of hours, maybe. I'll have to check our supplies first.'

'But if we helped you,' said Neville, 'we could get it done much quicker, right?'

There was a slight jolt in Zentalver's posture, a micro twitch across his head and shoulders, then he said, 'Gentlemen, please, you are in no state to be indulging in physical labour. I can see that you're both tired. I insist that you get some rest, and I'll carry out the work as quickly as possible.'

'OK. Thank you so much,' said Neville.

'The sleeping quarters are just through there,' said Zentalver, raising his hand in a smooth motion towards a set of automatic doors. 'Please get some sleep.'

And with that, the droid turned and walked away, leaving them to their own devices.

$$\triangle\triangle\triangle$$

They remained in the recreation suite for some time after Zentalver left, gorging themselves on frozen microwave food and discussing their situation.

'You've got to feel a little bit sorry for him really, haven't you?' said Neville, looking around at the shiny, immaculate surfaces of the room.

'What?' said Shane.

'You've got to feel sorry for Zentalver. The crew has obviously abandoned him and left him alone on this ship, and yet he still carries out his duties everyday, cleaning and maintaining.'

'How can you feel sorry for a droid? It

doesn't have any emotions.'

'Oh, OK, Shane, I'm not getting into this argument with you again. I just—'

'And how do you know they've abandoned him, anyway? They could be orbiting the ship in lifepods, just like he said.'

'Well, I didn't see them. Did you?'

'No, but that doesn't mean that they're not out there. And if they are out there, still in orbit, it could mean that we're in danger.'

'Why?'

'Because there could be a serious electrical fault on this vessel. If the crew haven't returned yet, it could be because they know that it's not safe to return.'

'Yeah, maybe. I didn't think of it like that. I'm more concerned about what our commanding officer will have to say to us when we get back.'

'And who's fault is that, Neville? You're the one who got us into this mess!'

'I'm fully aware of that, thank you. You don't have to keep reminding me.'

'The Sprintjet's comms system is probably going crazy already. We're going to have to go down there soon and reply to some—'

'I've disabled it.'

'You've what?!'

'I switched off the communication system just before docking. I'm not ready to speak to anyone back at base yet. I've screwed up Shane, and I'm not sure what I'm going to say to them. I can't just admit that I left without emergency fuel. I could get executed for that if the CO's having a bad day.'

'And you think switching off the comms system is going to help?'

'It'll look like we've experienced a technical issue. When we get back to base we can say that the ship was malfunctioning. We'll say that the navigation system and the comms system went down, which will explain both the loss of time and communication.'

'For some reason,' growled Shane, 'you keep on saying "we". This is *your* fuck up, Neville, and *you're* going to be the one who does the explaining, not me!'

'That's fine. I wouldn't expect you to help me out, anyway,' snarled Neville.

'Well, why should I?'

'We're supposed to be partners, work colleagues, that's why.'

'Oh yeah? If work colleagues are supposed to look out for each other, why the hell are you taking us both out without emergency fuel?'

Neville shot up to his feet, shaking his head in frustration. 'Oh, whatever! I'm too tired to be dealing with you.'

'At last, we feel the same way about something.'

Neville mumbled some obscenity then stormed out of the recreation suite, distancing himself from his intolerable work colleague. He didn't have a clue where he was going, he just needed to walk and cool off.

Neville was scared, and the last thing he wanted was Shane digging away at him. He was walking down a long corridor, taking deep breaths in an effort to calm his nerves, not really thinking about where he was heading to. When a thick set of doors appeared up ahead of him, he suddenly realised that he'd inadvertently walked to the end of one of the five long columns of the ship. He stopped mid-stride, feeling as though he was about to intrude on something, like he shouldn't be there, but at the same time he was very curious as to what was on the other side of the big heavy doors. *Wanis* was a research vessel, he knew that, but he didn't know what kind of research went on here. There was nobody around, no sign of anybody, and as far as he knew Zentalver was down in the docking station working on the Sprintjet. Silently and tentatively, he crept towards the doors.

The sight that confronted him on the other side took his breath away. The biggest laboratory he'd ever seen was stretched out before him, with sophisticated-looking instruments and utensils filling every inch of the room. The chrome tanks, test tubes, beakers, measuring cylinders, syringes and microscopes gleamed and sparkled under the crisp overhead lighting, projecting a strange kind of beauty.

Naturally, he began to explore the lab, gazing around at all of the displays and contraptions, and it didn't take long for him to find some peculiar-looking samples and specimens. A rack of test tubes sitting on one of the side tables were filled with a variety of murky liquids and solutions, and nearby on a separate worktop a set of glass microscope slides displayed wafer-thin segments of some kind of organic matter that Neville couldn't identify.

Looking around at these oddities, he momentarily forgot about the trouble he'd gotten himself and Shane into, lost instead in the mystery of what the crew might've been studying. A plethora of speculations and ideas ran through his mind as he went from jar to jar, and test tube to test tube, but all of his thoughts and musings were sucked out of him as his eyes landed on a certain plastic display case. He was suddenly looking at the most hideous thing he'd ever seen, a dark specimen sealed inside the square, see-through case, floating in a clear solution. The sheer sight of it sent shivers running up and down Neville's spine, activating some primordial instinct within him. It was fairly small, its leg span only around an inch or so, but its ghastly structure and anatomy more than made up for its lack of size. It looked like a cross between a spider and some kind of prehistoric trilobite, its ribbed body flanked by jagged, barbed legs. It was ugly, to say the least, but the word *ugly* wasn't strong enough to describe this creature's appearance. *Vicious* was better, but even this wasn't quite strong enough. Neville had seen pictures of insects from Earth that'd creeped him out before, but this thing made spiders, trilobites, scorpions and millipedes all seem cuddly and pretty in comparison. It was hostility and danger encapsulated in physical form.

He couldn't stop himself, however, from crouching down and leaning towards it to get a better view, urged on by morbid fascination. He put his face as far up to the glass as he dared, studying the fierce little grooves and ridges on its body. His entire vision was filled with the black pointy limbs of this monster, this insect-like beast, when something moved across the glass.

'Our best specimen,' came a voice from over his shoulder.

'Whhooaaa!'

Neville jumped so much he almost fell to the floor. The movement across the glass had been Zentalver's reflection; somehow, he'd entered the room without him hearing.

'You...You scared the life out of me.'

'I do apologise. Are you OK?'

'Yes, I'm...I'm OK,' replied Neville, between heavy breaths. 'What the hell *is* this thing?'

'This is the main focus of our expedition. A parasite; yet to be named.'

'It's...It's grotesque.'

'That's how most humans seem to feel about it.'

'Where does it come from?'

'It comes from a moon of Jupiter. Earth space agencies became aware of its presence after a number of landings there some years ago.'

'Is *Wanis* owned by one of the major space agencies?'

'No,' said Zentalver. '*Wanis* is a private vessel.'

'A private research ship?'

'Yes. This ship, and this whole project, is owned and run by Professor Tatsfield, who has the means and motivation to pursue the things that interest him.'

'And he's out there in one of those lifepods, I take it?'

'Yes, he was required to evacuate the ship with the rest of the crew.'

'So what's so special about this parasite?' asked Neville, turning his attention back towards it.

'Professor Tatsfield is interested in its apparent ability to keep its host alive for abnormal amounts of time. It lives and feeds off of a variety of different organisms, extending their lifespans for its own benefit.'

'How does it do it?'

'We don't know yet. That's what the professor wants to find out.'

'Why is he so desperate to find this out?'

'So that he can extract whatever chemical this creature produces, and use it on himself.'

'He wants to extend his own lifespan?'

'Precisely.'

'How many of these things do you have on board?' asked Neville, looking across the vast lab.

'Several,' replied Zentalver, after a short pause.

After mulling all of this over in his head, Neville felt even more creeped out than he was before. He'd seen enough of this ship now, and he wanted to get off of it. 'Erm, is the Sprintjet refuelled yet, Zentalver?'

'No, I'm afraid not. That's why I came to look for you. I found some fuel onboard that you're welcome to make use of, but it's firmly stashed away in the cargo hold. It's going to take me a while to transport it over to the docking station.'

'How long?' asked Neville, nervously.

'Around three or four hours. May I again suggest that you get some rest while I set about doing it? You're more than welcome to use the facilities in the sleeping quarters.'

Neville groaned. Erilon officials would be looking for him by now, alerted to his absence. Some kind of severe punishment would await him on his return, and with this in mind he doubted that he'd be able to sleep. He also doubted that he'd be able to relax at all with the knowledge that this parasite was on the ship with him, but, despite all of this, there wasn't really much choice available to him.

Thanking Zentalver once again for his help and assistance, he exited the lab and made his way towards the sleeping quarters.

△△△

Neville and Shane were lying on opposite bunks in the sleeping quarters. Shane had managed to drift off into a deep sleep, but Neville was still wide awake, his bloodshot eyes staring blearily through the darkness. There was something not right about the *Wanis* vessel, something that didn't add up, and it was nagging away at him. Random items belonging to the missing crew were sitting around here and there: folded uniforms, combs, books, pens, pencils, cups and plates. There was even a dealt pack of cards laid out on a small table in the corner, with a few chips scattered around. An electrical fault had forced them all to evacuate? This seemed plausible at first, but something was now telling him that it wasn't true. For the last two hours he'd been looking out through a small window next to his bunk, a circular observation hatch pointing out towards the star-studded vista outside, and he'd seen absolutely no sign whatsoever of any of the six lifepods that were supposed to be orbiting the ship. Something was wrong.

Pushing the thin bedsheets away from him, he decided to get up and have another walk around.

He couldn't lie awake like this anymore, stewing and speculating about the quagmire he'd landed himself in, as well as the whereabouts of the crew. Creeping as quietly as he could, he made his way back through to the recreation suite and the adjoining lift. The automatic lighting system blinked to life as he stepped across the polished floor, and he squinted his eyes to adjust to the harsh glow. There were still four long arms of the ship that he could've explored, but he wanted to see what Zentalver was up to first, so he jumped in the elevator to travel down to a lower floor of the central body.

He couldn't quite remember whether the docking station was on the ground floor or the first floor, so he pressed the first floor button as a guess. When the doors opened a few minutes later he instantly knew that he'd chosen the wrong floor, but the sight that he was greeted by was so peculiar that he was unable to stop himself from walking out to get a closer look. Rows of tall white tanks lined a big room straight ahead of him, giving off an ominous, deep hum. Neville had stumbled upon a storage room of some kind, and he gingerly walked around to take a look.

The tanks were actually freezers, and each one had a dial and a digital display. His initial presumption was that the crew's food and drink supplies were kept here, mainly the microwave food that he and Shane had dined on earlier, and this indeed appeared to be correct when he pulled one of the big doors open and looked inside. Rows of frozen ready meals were stacked up high, enough to keep the crew nourished for months. Sealing the unit back up again, he walked on and looked around at some others. There were twenty or so altogether, all sitting there in the dim light humming away. He opened another unit, then another, eyeing up the various contents. Some had tubs of ice cream in them, some had yogurt, and others just had large bags full of ice cubes.

After becoming bored of finding the same thing, Neville turned to head back to the elevator. Some dust markings in front of one of the tanks caught his eye, however, and he stopped to take a look. A thin layer of dust covered most of the freezer room floor, with footprints marking the ground here and there, but in front of this particular freezer the footprints were more prominent. There were other markings, too, where something had been dragged or scraped across the ground, and upon seeing this sign of disturbance Neville simply had to open up the unit to see what it contained.

A cloud of icy mist drifted out towards him as he opened the door, and he stood there for a while as it cleared. After a few seconds, when he could see clearly into the big compartment, his chin dropped to the floor in shock. He was looking at a white, icy bundle, arranged neatly at the back of the freezer unit. Heads, faces, torsos and limbs jutted out of the huge ice block like fallen logs in an arctic storm, all coated with a thin layer of frost. Bloodied stumps sat atop sliced shoulder blades, arms and hands were piled up like sticks, and sections of chopped abdomen were placed around like veal.

The whole thing was too vulgar to be real —that's what Neville told himself, anyway. But once the initial shock subsided and his brain kicked back into gear, he knew that what he was looking at was very real indeed. He also knew, with no doubt whatsoever, that the mutilated carcasses belonged to the missing crew. And if that was the case, Neville thought, there could only be one possible culprit: Zentalver. The droid had obviously malfunctioned in some major way, a glitch in its circuitry causing it to go haywire, and it would have to be shut down and destroyed as soon as possible.

After sealing the freezer unit back up, Neville sprinted to the lift and pressed the button for the recreation suite. He needed to wake Shane up and alert him to what was going on.

Shane was in the midst of a bizarre dream when he was abruptly shaken awake.

'Shane! Get up! Something's not right!'

'Uh? What the hell are you doing?' he said, leaning up on the bunk with his hair wildly askew.

'The droid's malfunctioned! It's fucking dangerous! It's murdered the entire fucking crew! Come on, we need to get off this fucking ship right now!'

'What? How do you know this?'

'I've just found the crew,' said Neville, chucking Shane's clothes at him. 'They're all sliced up. Stashed away in a giant freezer like piles of frozen meat.'

There was a moment of uncertainty as Shane gaped over the edge of the bunk, trying to gauge whether he was still dreaming or not. His mouth hung slack with sleep saliva drooling from his gums, and his red eyes struggled to focus.

'Freezer? Why are they in a freezer?'

'Because Zentalver put them there, that's why! Just get dressed, we need to go!'

'So where's Zentalver now?'

'I don't know, I didn't see him. As soon as

I found the dead crew, I came straight back up here to come and get you.'

Shane, now awake, leapt down from his bunk and threw on his clothes. 'I knew there was something wrong with that droid.'

'Let's just get back down to the Sprintjet, shall we?'

'What if it's down there waiting for us?'

'I don't know,' shrugged Neville. 'We just need to get away from this place.'

The two of them ran out of the sleeping quarters towards the lift, lost in a world of panic.

As the lift grinded to a halt on the ground floor, they both braced themselves. They didn't know what they were going to be confronted with, and their nerves were racing.

'We should have grabbed a knife or something from the recreation suite,' whispered Neville, feeling completely defenceless.

'Too late,' muttered Shane, as the doors began to slowly open.

Their worst fear, the worst possible scenario, came into fruition before their very eyes. Zentalver was standing directly outside the lift in his beige spacesuit, just a few feet away from them, and he began to walk forward with his mechanical stride. Neville was closest to the elevator's controls but he was caught in a daze, stunned by blind fear and terror.

'Close the doors! Now!' screamed Shane.

'Huh?'

'Press a button! Just press any fucking button!'

Snapping himself out of his stupefaction, Neville pressed a button at random and the doors closed again. As soon as Zentalver's bulky form had vanished, Shane looked over towards the illuminated button panel.

'What floor are we going to?'

'Second,' said Neville. 'Do you know what's up there?'

'Not a clue,' replied Shane, with a desperate shake of his head.

As it happened, the second floor was used as another storage area, although this one was not for frozen goods. A long circular corridor was lined with dozens of small rooms and cupboards, and upon brief inspection most of them were filled with tools, clothing or laboratory equipment. They both swiftly armed themselves up with crowbars and hammers, then, standing a safe distance away from the elevator doors, tried to come up with a decent plan of action. A noise distracted them from further down the corridor, however, and they both turned to look.

'What was that?' Neville asked.

'I don't know. It sounded like someone shouting.'

Creeping along stealthily, they followed the

muffled noise. After a few minutes they could see that it was coming from behind one of the locked cupboard doors, and they stopped to investigate.

They immediately noticed that this door was very different from the others, as it had been tampered with and modified. A small hatch had been cut out of the bottom section, and an extra lock had also been fitted. A male voice bellowed out from behind the door, screaming and pleading.

'Help me! Help me, please!'

They both looked down towards the small rectangular hatch at the bottom of the door, roughly the same size as a dinner plate, then met each others' eyes with a knowing look. Someone was being kept prisoner in this small, reinforced cupboard.

'Who are you?' Shane shouted, towards the crack of the door.

'My...My name is Tatsfield. Professor Tatsfield,' came the distressed voice.

'Oh, no! I don't believe it!' said Neville.

'What? What is it?'

'Professor Tatsfield! He's the one who organised this entire expedition. He owns the damn ship!'

'Help me! Please open the door!' continued the voice.

'How do you know all of this?' asked Shane.

'Oh, it doesn't matter. Just mind out, and let

me get this lock off,' replied Neville, wedging his crowbar against the mechanism.

Using all of his weight, he pushed and pulled against the lock until it came crunching off and dropped to the floor. When the door swung open a potent wave of body odour hit them both in the face, causing them to wince and gag. The professor had obviously been locked away in the room for a very long time, and it showed on his physical appearance, too. Dressed in just a white T-shirt and shorts, his thin body trembled with a mixture of fear and malnourishment, and half of his face was hidden by a wild, messy beard. His grey eyes were sunken pits of manic despair, and as Neville and Shane looked into the room, which was empty apart from a manky-looking mattress and some old plates, he resembled a tormented animal that'd been thrown into a cage and forgotten about.

'Who...Who are you?' he said.

Shane gave the man a quick rundown of who they were and how they'd ended up on the ship.

'We...We need to shut down the droid. It's gone haywire!' said Tatsfield, glaring over at them with a row of rotten teeth showing through the strands of his beard.

'How do we do it?' said Neville.

'There's...There's an emergency immobiliser switch down on the ground floor. If we can get to it, we can shut him down.'

'OK, show us where it is then.'

'But Zentalver is down on the ground floor,' interrupted Shane. 'If—'

'Urgh! Please don't mention that name!' cried the professor. 'It doesn't deserve a name! It's a faulty piece of machinery, that's all. A piece of junk that's ready for the scrap heap.'

'Look,' said Neville, 'we're armed now. It'd be better if we had guns, but at least we've got something. He might not even be down there anymore, anyway.'

With no other choice available to them, Shane conceded.

Tatsfield was in a state as the three of them walked along the corridor. The light was hurting his eyes, and he lacked the strength to carry himself along properly. He looked like he'd just stumbled out of a hospital somewhere.

'How long have you been locked up in that room?' asked Neville, watching him painfully hobble
along.

'I really couldn't say,' groaned Tatsfield. 'But it feels like years.'

When the lift doors opened up on the ground floor, Neville gripped his crowbar tightly and Shane raised his hammer up above his head. The professor cowered at the back of the lift, trembling like a traumatised child.

They were greeted with nothing but silence, however, and after a few hesitant moments they all stepped out.

'The...The switch is this way,' the professor whispered over their shoulders. 'It's located in the droid's charging station.'

Tatsfield directed them across platforms and corridors, traipsing along between them for protection, until a loud bang in the distance caused them all to stop.

'What was that?' said Neville.

Shane turned his head in the direction of the docking station behind them. 'I don't know, but it came from down near the Sprintjet. I'm going to go and take a look.'

Neville and the professor watched as he walked over to the entrance of the docking station, peered in, then came back with a bewildered look on his face.

'Well?' whispered Neville.

'He's...*It's* fixing the Sprintjet,' Shane said, frowning.

Neville pondered this for a moment, shrugged, and said, 'Well, let's just leave him to it. Professor, show us where this switch is.'

They continued along the grated walkways, as silently as they could, until Tatsfield pointed to a steel chamber.

'H...Here,' he stuttered. 'This is it.'

Zentalver's charging station looked retro-futuristic. It was unnecessary in its complexity, with tangles of sockets, terminals and attachments hanging from all four walls. If there was any doubt in Neville and Shane's mind that *Wanis* was an earth-built vessel, it vanished completely upon seeing this outdated, borderline embarrassing piece of technology.

'The droid has to plug itself into this to recharge?' said Shane. 'Seems a bit outdated.'

'I...I funded this entire ship myself,' said Tatsfield, looking away. 'I had to budget and distribute my money carefully. I simply couldn't afford to build a top of the range maintenance droid.'

Boy, did that come back and bite you in the ass, thought Neville, biting his tongue.

'I'm guessing that's the immobiliser switch?' said Shane, looking up at a big red lever on the wall.

'Yes, that's it,' croaked the professor. 'Pull it down.'

Shane pulled the big lever down, a wry grin spread across his face as he did so. There was no satisfying noise, though, nothing that indicated anything had actually happened. 'Is that it? Do I have to do anything else?'

'No, that's it. We're safe now,' said Tatsfield, his bearded face slackening with relief for the first time since leaving his cell.

'Let's take a look at the Sprintjet,' said Neville.

Everyone nodded in agreement, then took

off.

The sight of Zentalver crouched down next to the Sprintjet, still and unmoving, had a strange effect on everyone. Neville, for one, despite witnessing the mutilated remains of the crew firsthand, couldn't help but feel sympathetic towards him. There was something about the droid's pose, something about the way he was frozen in position, that made him appear pitiful.

An array of thoughts span through Neville's mind as they all made their way down the steel staircase towards the Sprintjet: *the robot is an evil killer. But no, that can't be true. It malfunctioned, probably due to a technical hitch in its wiring or software, so it can't be held responsible. A technical hitch means that there's no evil intent within the droid's artificial mind. But then again, if a human being with a mental illness kills someone, they're still held responsible. Or are they? Can a robot ever be guilty? Can a robot ever feel, or understand guilt?* Neville snapped himself out of his philosophical musings as he felt himself get carried away. He was tired, exhausted, and the ordeal was still far from over. He'd have plenty of time to think about this stuff back on Erilon —providing he wasn't executed for this colossal fuck up of his.

'Don't get too close to it,' said Shane. 'It might start moving again for all we know.'

Looking at Zentalver leaning over his pile of tools was like looking at a photograph or a movie still. It was eerie and unsettling. The professor, however, felt confident that they were safe.

'No, the immobiliser has worked. It would never become that still, otherwise. Even if its battery was critically low, it would still have some kind of movement.'

As these words sank in, Shane marched over to the droid's motionless form and stamped a heel in its back, making it topple and roll over. It rocked back and forth for a few seconds, its hard body rattling the steel grated floor, then came to rest like a discarded toy figurine, its arms and legs jutting out at awkward angles. Neville watched this with gritted teeth, but kept his objections to himself. The important issue right now was getting the Sprintjet up and running, and thankfully it looked as though Zentalver had finished refuelling it.

'We just need to get this cover screwed back on, and we can get the hell out of here,' spat Shane, stepping over Zentalver's fallen body.

'Yes,' agreed Neville. 'But, err, what are we going to do with the droid?'

'That's not for me to decide,' said Shane, sternly. 'Nor is it for you to decide.'

'What do you mean?'

'I mean that you're going to climb up into that cockpit, switch the comms system back on, and then follow whatever orders are given to you.'

'But—'

'Just do it, Neville. Tell them exactly what's happened, then let them decide what they want to do. Let's not make things worse than they already are.'

'What are they going to do with the professor? What's going to happen to him?'

Shane turned towards Tatsfield, lowering his voice slightly. 'Professor, we have to follow procedure from here on. My guess is that the officials on Erilon will try to get some kind of payment from the relevant authorities on Earth, then they'll send you back unharmed. Money means more to them than anything else, and I'm sure the kind folks back on Earth will pay up.' Turning back to Neville, he said, 'Explain to them that the professor is a victim here. Tell them that he's been locked in a damn cupboard for god knows how long. They might even show a bit of sympathy and compassion towards him. Stranger things have happened'

Looking like a condemned man on his way to the gallows, Neville walked towards the cockpit, ready to face the music.

△△△

'Wow!' said Shane, wiping his brow. 'It's a

lot heavier than it looks.'

Neville simply nodded in response, too out of breath to speak. The three of them—Tatsfield included, despite his insistence that they simply eject the faulty droid out into space—had just finished lifting Zentalver up into the Sprintjet's cargo hold, which was barely big enough to contain him.

Neville had bravely made the call to Erilon, and, after being subjected to the anticipated questioning and stern warnings, he'd been ordered to return back to base bringing both the professor and the robot. After the call Tatsfield had asked what they planned on doing with him, and Neville had assured him that there was absolutely nothing to worry about. He explained that they had no intention of punishing him or detaining him, but if the truth be told he wasn't so sure. The Erilonian superiors had not specified what they wanted to do with Tatsfield, but Neville needed him to be calm and cooperative until they got him back to Mars, so he simply told him what he wanted to hear.

'How much does that thing actually weigh, Professor?' asked Shane.

'About seventeen stone, if I remember rightly.'

'It felt more like twenty to me.'

'I told you we'd be better off getting rid of it.'

'Look, it's done now,' said Neville. 'Let's just go, shall we?'

Tatsfield hesitated before climbing up into the Sprintjet, looking around the interior of the large room with a sadness in his eyes. 'What's going to happen to my ship? And...'

'Everything will be recovered in due course,' said Neville. 'Our coordinates were taken while I made the call, and they're now tracking both vessels.'

The professor, who still looked severely ill and malnourished, gave a weak nod.

'Come on, Tatsfield,' said Shane, guiding the professor towards the cockpit ladder. 'There's a ration pack up there with your name on it.'

Five minutes later, after they'd all climbed aboard and strapped themselves in, they were hurtling through the darkness of space towards the Red Planet.

PART 2

When the tiny speck of light appeared on the martian horizon, Neville knew exactly what it was. He could see it clearly from his cell window, a piercing glow through the thick reinforced glass, and he watched on as it grew in size and luminosity. After three months of incarceration he felt isolated and detached from his fellow Erilonians, but despite this segregation certain rumours and snippets of news still reached him through the prison walls. As he'd predicted, a large sum of money had been demanded for the safe return of Tatsfield and the broken droid, and this bright speck that he could see in the distance was an Earth vessel on its way to pick them up.

Neville felt a surprising amount of sentimentality as the incoming ship drew closer, descending down towards the martian soil. He knew that he would never see Professor Tatsfield again after he departed for Earth, and despite only having known the man for the briefest amount of time, his impact on him had been strong nonetheless. Stronger still, though, was the impact that the droid had made on him. Zentalver had given off the impression of ultimate sophistication and manners, but a dark secret had been hiding away underneath that veneer of innocence, a secret so sinister Neville doubted he would ever be the same again. *What had caused the robot to kill? Why did it spare Professor Tatsfield's life, but kill everybody else? Why did it stash the crews' bodies in the freezers, in an apparent attempt to preserve them?*

These were the thoughts that ran through Neville's mind every night as he lay on his cell bed, deep within the walls of the martian prison.

ΔΔΔ

The atmosphere was tense in the prime minister's office. A huge amount of UK taxpayers' money had been spent retrieving Professor Tatsfield from Mars, as well as recovering his private vessel, but now it appeared as though the ordeal was not yet over.

'It could prove to be very beneficial to us, sir,' said Mr Greyridge, the PM's chief science advisor. 'If we could find out what went wrong with that robot, we could prevent anything like this from happening during one of our own agency's space missions.'

'I don't want to spend any more money on this! The elections are coming up, and the press are all over me.'

'The software that the professor used for his

robot is similar to what we use for some of our maintenance robots. Imagine what the press would say if we ignored this and—'

'Hasn't the professor hinted that he might've badly programmed the bloody thing? We wouldn't make mistakes like that. He wants it destroyed as well, doesn't he? I mean, if he wants it destroyed, what's the point in—'

'Professor Tatsfield is not in a sound frame of mind, sir. We can't just accept his word on things.'

'Where is he now, anyway?'

'Tatsfield is being treated and cared for in a local hospital just a few miles from here. He's displaying signs of severe mental distress, but the doctors say that he should be able to make a full recovery in due course.'

The PM paced around his office for a few moments, running a hand through his hair and gazing out towards the window. 'OK,' he sighed. 'I'll make sure you get some funding to study the robot. Prevention is better than cure. We don't want anything like this happening on one of our own missions.'

'Thank you, sir. It's the right thing to do. I'll gather a team of technicians and engineers, and we'll find out exactly what went wrong.'

∆∆∆

Zentalver was spread out on a big steel table within one of the top governmental research facilities in London, his beige spacesuit stripped away to reveal his cumbersome body which was drained of all power. A small team of specialist technicians were in the room with him, relaxed in the knowledge that he was completely inert and out of service. They'd been hitting dead ends so far. The droid's software had been completely scanned for bugs and viruses, its circuitry had been examined for loose connections, and it's hardware had been checked for faults and dodgy fittings, but nothing was amiss. The only thing left to examine now was its memory. Everything Zentalver had ever seen since being switched on for the first time had been recorded through his synthetic eyes, then burned on to his internal memory, so the technicians were now focusing on the footage available to them. A large screen was fixed up on the wall, all ready and powered up.

The head technician cleared his throat and spoke to the room. 'There's going to be endless footage on here that we're going to have to sit through, boring, mundane footage of the droid cleaning and maintaining sections of the ship, but for now let's just try to find the part of the tape that shows the actual murders. That's what we need to do first.'

The man at the controls, sitting on a swivel

chair next to Zentalver's head, did as he was told and started to skim through large sections of tape. Years' worth of footage flashed across the monitor, and then the technician pressed the play button. An image of the Erilonian Sprintjet filled the screen, as seen from Zentalver's point of view as he paced around trying to refuel it.

'Too far,' said the head tech. 'Back up a little bit.'

Rewinding the tape a little, Zentalver was then seen pushing a tray of food through a small hatch in a cupboard door.

'Back it up some more.'

Around ten minutes or so was spent going backwards and forwards, rewinding and fast-forwarding the tape, as they looked for the precise moment when Zentalver attacked and killed the crew.

'Whoa! Stop right there!' shouted the head tech, when a wave of scarlet washed across the screen.

A couple of faces went pale as the team watched the monitor, which now displayed *Wanis's* recreation suite. The scene was worse than a nightmare. As Zentalver turned his head left and right, apparently to survey and admire his handiwork, an array of freshly killed bodies could be seen sprawled across the tiled floor, with pools of thick blood glistening in between them. Deep stab wounds punctured flesh, limbs were ripped apart, and bone protruded from stumps. The room's bright fluorescent lighting exposed every grizzly detail of the massacre, presenting it to the technicians in glorious, vivid technicolour. A couple of them looked down at Zentalver in disgust, wondering how anyone or anything, human or machine, could be capable of carrying out such a thing.

'Rewind some more, please,' said the head, struggling to keep himself composed in the face of this macabre recording.

Blurred colours and images whizzed across the big screen, then, all of a sudden, the crew were alive and well, going about their tasks.

'Let's play it from here.'

The camera showed various members of the *Wanis* vessel brushing past Zentalver as he walked among them, but the footage then shifted to an empty corridor. They all watched on as the droid spent some time repairing a faulty light, before returning back to the re-creation suite. Everyone studied the monitor closely, eyes peeled, bracing themselves for the dreaded moment. A set of double doors came into view as Zentalver walked along, a corner was turned, and then...

'What? What the hell? He didn't touch them! Why are they dead?'

The entire team looked at each other, the answer forming in their heads with a flash of horror.

'Oh, shit!' cried the head technician. 'Somebody call the hospital! Now!'

Professor Tatsfield looked calm as he sat there in the canteen area of the hospital, surrounded by the chatter and murmurings of his fellow diners. His clean-shaven cheeks revealed a neutral expression, free from any signs of distress, but inside his mind things were very different. The nurses were well aware of Tatsfield's occasional mood swings and unpredictable behaviour, but he was granted complete freedom to wander around the premises nonetheless. Trauma victims always behaved this way, and it was to be expected from someone who'd suffered such a great ordeal. The doctors had dealt with countless patients suffering from post traumatic stress, so they were more than familiar with this kind of thing. They were so accustomed to it, in fact, that the idea of scanning the professor's head for anomalies hadn't occurred to anyone. This was a tragic shame, as well as a neglect of medical duties, because if they'd taken the time to do so they would've found the parasite lodged deep within the folds of his grey matter, gnawing away at his neural connections.

The organism had been lying dormant for quite some time now, burrowed away comfortably in the warmth of its host, but now it was beginning to stir. It needed its host to stay alive for as long as possible, providing it with a stable home, so it began to secrete its chemical cocktail liberally.

Tatsfield's cells were being rejuvenated and replenished as he hunched over the canteen dinner table, his veins flowing with an extraterrestrial life-preserving liquid, but it would soon have a very potent effect on his psyche. Jupiter's moons carry a wide range of life forms, all brutal and savage, carving out lives for themselves in a harsh, unforgiving terrain. Only the violent, hardy and bloodthirsty survive in Jupiter's orbit, and so a psychosis-inducing chemical cocktail always gives an advantage.

A trembling started to erupt across Tatsfield's features as he gazed across the dining area, his fingers whitening around his knife. The patients and visitors sitting around him began to morph and alter in appearance the more he looked at them, taking on different forms and shapes. The half-eaten plate of food in front of him was forgotten as a cloud of red mist engulfed him, making him dizzy with rage and hate. Strange urges were welling up inside of him, primal, reptilian urges. When he finally gave in, succumbing to his animalistic desire, he looked like a creature from another world, as alien as the organism wedged between the walls of his cranium. Within seconds his dinner knife was dripping with blood, innocent bodies dropping like sacks of meat. He lashed out like a wild beast, slicing arteries and gauging faces with sick gusto, thrashing and dancing about the place as though controlled by an invisible hand.

Sirens rose up from somewhere outside, along with panicked voices out in the wards, but none of it mattered. He was alive, that was all that mattered, a live host for the puppet master in his brain.

THE END

Did you enjoy this book? Yes? Well, why not grab a microphone and shout about it in the street?

Too much? Okay, why not leave a review for it on Amazon or Goodreads instead?

It'll help more than you think.

Made in the USA
Columbia, SC
26 April 2020

94120804R00183